Bethan Jones has a passion for history and writing. She has always been fascinated by the legend of Robin Hood, which led her to research medieval history and from there has developed a love for visiting historic sites. This and her imagination have led her to write a new take on Robin Hood from a female perspective.

Bethan lives with chronic illnesses but does not let that stop her. Her writing distracts and transports her to a different world where she can delve into the lives of her characters.

For my wonderful parents who are there for me no matter what, and my grandma, Audrey, for being my biggest fan.

For my late grandad, Selwyn, who showed me I could achieve anything, and for all those living with chronic illness. This book is proof that sometimes your dreams can come true.

Bethan Jones

MARIAN

AUSTIN MACAULEY PUBLISHERS™

LONDON ★ CAMBRIDGE ★ NEW YORK ★ SHARJAH

A CIP catalogue record for this title is available from the British Library.

ISBN 9781398415317 (Paperback)
ISBN 9781398415324 (ePub e-book)

www.austinmacauley.com

First Published 2022
Austin Macauley Publishers Ltd®
1 Canada Square
Canary Wharf
London
E14 5AA

I would like to thank my parents, Gill and Gareth for being the most incredible, supportive people in the world and putting up with my crazy imagination. Thanks to my family and friends for listening to my ramblings about Marian and sharing in my excitement. I cannot forget the random people I met on holidays to the Canary Islands who were interested in my writing and helped expand some of my ideas when this book was in its early stages. Finally, I'd like to thank my wonderful partner Simon for always supporting my dreams.

Chapter 1

Marian awoke before dawn. It was Saturday – Market Day! Beatrice rushed in to dress her as she did every morning, with only a candle for light. Marian preferred it that way; it hid the scars across her back. She shivered as memories stirred of a life forgotten by all except Marian. The secrets she had left behind still haunted her to this day.

"It is meant to be a lovely day, Marian. I hear the market will be busy," Beatrice said. Beatrice always interrupted silence, though Marian longed for it sometimes. When Marian first arrived in Nottingham, Beatrice had been the first person she met. She was the only one Marian trusted to see her true form. Even Walter, the Sheriff of Nottingham, the kindly man who saved her from her past, didn't know she still bore the scars.

"I had best be off then," Marian replied. She left hastily, lifting the hood of her cloak. She always dressed down when venturing into town. To everyone else, she could be anybody. Nobody knew what she looked like, only gossiped that she was a recluse, a crazy man-hater. Women were not meant to live alone, but Walter had allowed her to, as long as she had maids to help her. When she arrived in Nottingham, she had lived in the castle for a while, but begged Walter to let her live away; she could not bear having people staring at her all the time, or the guards around every corner. She could never be at peace in such a place. It had been like moving from one prison to another. Of course, she had never been to a real gaol, but what she had endured in her youth had been far worse.

Every day, no matter how hard she tried, something would remind her of the past she would prefer to forget. Today it had been the small talk with Beatrice. It took her back years, to when she had made friends with Meggy, a maid in her uncle's manor. When Marian's mother had died, her father could not cope. He sent her away to live with an uncle she never knew existed. He had been crueller than she had ever imagined a person could be, forcing her to be somebody she could never be. Her mother had brought her up to be kind and caring, but also intelligent and brave; qualities that men despised in women. She had never learnt to hide it, and her uncle had wanted to sell her off for marriage to a wealthy family. He whipped her every day for the year she lived with him, until she finally escaped.

Meggy had been the only person in her uncle's manor to show her kindness. She was a gossip, like Beatrice, but Meggy had snuck her out every morning to have some time to herself in the forest that surrounded the manor. It was the only thing that had kept Marian sane, all those years ago.

Now Marian walked along the brightening streets, everyone still in bed, but the baker.

Every Wednesday, Marian collected the first batch of baked goods to come out of the baker's oven. The baker had never been told who she was, and he had never seen her face. A couple of years ago, the taxes had increased, and Walter had no choice but to obey, as the order had come from King Richard himself. Marian had seen the people suffer through it and asked Beatrice to make a deal with the baker to leave his fresh food out to be collected every Wednesday. Beatrice paid him a monthly fee for the service. As Marian approached it today, she tucked a straying brown hair into the hood of her cloak and looked around cautiously. As usual, nobody was around, and she took the basket quickly, rushing off in the opposite direction, her heart racing.

Marian continued through the deserted streets, walking to the poorer area of Nottingham. She placed food outside a few of the poorest homes until she ran out. She saved a small piece of bread for herself, to eat on her way to the castle.

Marian never liked to take the direct route to the castle. Instead, she ventured to the outskirts of Nottingham, on the border to the forest. She sat on a tree stump and ate her bread. To her, the forest was a place of wonder and freedom. It was where outlaws lived, outside of any laws, free to choose their own paths in life. She knew it was only a romantic dream, that it was far from the dark truth, but the forest held the only positive memories of her past life, when she went by another name – Mary.

Every time, she sat on this very stump and longed for the freedom the forest had once given to her; when Meggy would let her out for an hour every morning before her uncle awoke. Mary would walk for as long as she could, until inevitably she would return to her uncle. She had taken the same path every day through the forest, not going anywhere for any one purpose. However, one fateful day, the anniversary of her mother's death, she had left earlier than usual, before even the first light had woken the wildlife. She had been tearful and weak, ready to leave forever. She had not known what to do, but she was ready to take her own life if she had to. She had walked and walked until she was no longer on her usual path. She had sat on a stump, not dissimilar to the one she sat on now, not able to hold in the pain anymore, and cried.

Even though she had been certain she was alone, she felt eyes on her. She had looked up and into another's eyes and screamed. He had cupped his hand over her mouth to quieten her. She was certain he would kill her. He held a dagger in his free hand and there was a quiver and arrows attached to his back. He wore green, as if he could blend in with the forest.

"Shh, you'll wake my gang," the boy whispered. "I will not harm you." He took his hand away slowly.

"Who are you?" she asked breathlessly, still very aware of his weapons. She had never learnt how to use a weapon and had nothing to defend herself with. But something in his eyes told her he was true to his word.

"My name is Robert, but everyone calls me Robin Hood, see?" He reached behind his back and pulled a green hood over his head. "I am a hero of the woods, fighting evil and rescuing damsels in distress." He pointed at Mary and she giggled. She had never known anyone the same age as herself before, and she realised what she had missed out on: imagination. She had been stuck in the same pattern for a year and had not laughed in all that time. She had lost sense of what it was like to be a child; now was the time to let go. She needed to enjoy this time while she had it.

"My name is Mary." She smiled, the first she had really meant in a very long time.

His eyes seemed to glow with a longing for mystery and adventure.

"You need a hero name like me! How about… how about Marian? Saviour of the poor, healer of the weak."

Marian remembered that feeling, like it was yesterday. The feeling of pure adventure and freedom, with endless possibilities. It had been her first and last taste of freedom.

Eventually, they had found their way back to the clearing where they first met. He sat on the same log and motioned for Mary to sit next to him. He suddenly seemed far away, focused on the distance, as if something troubled him.

"I am moving away tomorrow." And with that her fun had ended.

"But, but… I do not want to go back. I want to stay with you, have more adventures," her younger self pleaded. Her cheeks flushed at the memory. She would never show weakness like that today.

"Then come with me," he had replied. "I live with outlaws, they are like a family. We look out for each other. They will love you; I know they will. Tomorrow morning at sunrise, meet me in this spot."

Marian tried to stop the flashback at that moment. She hated that she always did this to herself, but the trauma of what had happened next would play on her mind for the rest of her life. Even though for years she had trained herself how to use a sword, a bow and arrow, knives – anything she could use as a weapon – she could not train herself to forget her past, to leave it where it belonged. It always stayed with her, an invisible shadow, linking her to her past forevermore.

She stood abruptly. She continued her walk to the castle. There was a flash of a whip behind her eyes as she blinked. She walked faster, not wanting to be alone with her thoughts any longer.

After that day, she had never seen Robin Hood again, but it was entwined in the bad memories and at least that was one part she did not want to forget. She could live with keeping that memory alive.

Marian finally arrived at Nottingham Castle. The sun shone high in the sky and the streets were getting busier as the day wore on. She lowered her hood; the guards knew what she looked like and let her through. Walter had sworn the guards to secrecy of Marian's identity and the fact she visited the castle. She had to keep the ruse to the rest of Nottingham, so they would not bother her. She hated being the centre of attention.

The castle was a dark place, with cold, grey walls and very little natural light entering through the tiny windows. She hated to feel so trapped. The castle held a gaol, but to her the whole place was one big prison. She walked straight to Walter's chambers, not wanting to linger in such a disturbing place. She knocked on the door.

"Come in." She opened the door to see Walter sat at his desk, eating porridge.

"How do you stomach that stuff?"

"If you would only try it…" He laughed as she made a face at the thought of eating such gruel. "I know you say you are not high born, but you have the taste of a queen."

"I do not know whether that is a compliment or an insult!"

"Have you been on your errands today?"

"Of course, as every Saturday. It is a beautiful day, please come to market with me."

"You know I always have too much work to do. How do you put up with me?" Marian did not want to answer that honestly. She knew he was only joking, but she could not imagine life without him. He had given her a new life. Without him, she probably would not be alive today.

"I love you father." She meant it. Her real father had meant nothing to her. Her mother had been the only one to care. Marian's father had always loved her mother, but he was indifferent to Mary. He had wanted a boy who could provide for his family, not 'a silly little girl who will bring nothing but more poverty to our family name'. Then when her mother had become ill, her father had blamed her even more, and even tried to sell her to a rich family to pay for medicine. But no medicine would have saved her mother. Her heart throbbed at the thought, and she fiddled with the necklace she had worn every day since her mother died. Her mother had given it to her, to remember her by. It was the only possession her mother had ever kept, even when they had become poor, she refused to sell it.

"Oh, darling," Walter sighed. He had always been able to read her feelings too well. "You are the bravest person I know. I love you too. You are a godsend to Nottingham as well. The people should know what you do for them."

"Please. You promised you would not reveal what I do."

"I do not understand you, Marian. I never have. But I will not go back on a promise. Just like I provide you with your weapons, and I pray you will never have need for them, but I am glad you are protected."

"What is troubling you?" She always knew when there was something on his mind. He was always careful with his expressions, but he kept his hands busy when he was anxious, and right now he was fiddling with some parchment.

"The usual. Prince John's constant threat against England. I am certain he will return to England soon and try to rule it while Richard is away fighting."

Walter was a harbinger of peace and equality between the people. When he and Marian had arrived in Nottingham, there were riots in the streets between the Normans and Saxons. Walter had worked hard to keep the peace, and now Nottingham felt like a community, much more united than any of the nearby cities and towns. The threat of Longchamp and Prince John weighed heavily on him; Nottingham was seen as a place of power by both sides and Walter did everything he could to stop a full out war in Nottingham. He often tried to hide his worries about the threat, but Marian had her ways of finding out, and she refused to be oblivious as to the politics, even though it was often uninspiring and words rarely turned into actions.

"But John is exiled, surely they will not let him back."

"You forget he is a prince. Anyway, you know too much for a Lady. Make sure you never speak such politics in front of a man."

"Yes, you have told me many times. Do not worry, if I should ever meet a man, I will be sure to act like a silly girl." She regretted her choice of words as soon as she said them. But he was always so protective over her. It seemed to be all he cared about, other than the concerns of Nottingham.

"So you will not join me in the market? I am sure the people will want to see you."

"You would risk being seen in public for me? Or would I go to the market alone, with you blending in with the crowd?"

"Sorry. I wish I could, but…"

"I know," he interrupted, gratefully, before she had to say anymore.

Marian ended up going to the market alone as usual. She walked home early afternoon to make some time for training. She could not help but feel like she was being watched as she entered her home, sweating and exhausted from hours of practicing with her sword.

Chapter 2

Running through the forest, the agony of the fresh wounds on my back threatening to end me. I look over my shoulder; I cannot hear or see anyone, but I know uncle is there, somewhere. I scratch my arms against trees as I carelessly run. My legs somehow carrying me away from the manor, not even sure how I have the energy. But where will I go? I have no idea where I am. I try not to think about it. As long as I am far from uncle, I will be fine.

My foot catches on a twig and I scrape my legs on the forest floor. I struggle to my feet again, my heart racing so hard I might pass out. One foot in front of the other. I have to make it. This is my only chance. I tumble into the clearing and recognise it instantly. This is where Robin told me to meet him. I freeze in horror; I am too late. The outlaws have left without me. Robin Hood had been true to his word. It was past dawn and they had moved on.

Rough arms grab me from behind and I know I am doomed. Uncle.

Marian awoke, gasping for air. That was not how it had ended. The thought of what might have been sent a shiver through her body. She took a minute to catch her breath, looking out the window.

It was early morning, with the sun beaming through her window. She rarely slept in, but the unease of the last few days had gotten to her. She spent hours at night watching the woods, growing increasingly aware someone was watching her. Something had woken her from her nightmare.

Marian shot out of bed as a crash echoed from downstairs. This was what she had prepared herself for. Instinctively, she grabbed her bow and slung the arrows in their sheath across her back. Marian had trained every day in every type of combat, from swords and knives to the bow and arrow. She knew she could defend herself from any situation, but this was the first time she had been tested. She had vowed never to be put in a defenceless position again, but she could not help but be afraid. In the back of her mind she always held the fear that her uncle would find her.

"Go on, get out of here! There is nothing worth taking!" Marian could hear Beatrice yell. Marian reached the top of the stairs and paused, examining the situation. She saw Beatrice by the servants' quarters, shielding Alice behind her. Beatrice had brought Alice to her about half a year ago, having found her alone on the outskirts of town. She was a traumatised young girl, reminding Marian much of herself at that age.

Marian counted seven intruders altogether, positioned around her upturned furniture, dressed in torn, green and brown clothes; outlaws. Most of them were searching to find anything of value but one had stopped and was looking directly at her, smirking.

Disgusting, Marian thought, *that a man could think he is superior to a woman. I cannot wait to see your face when I prove you wrong.* She smiled at him, a fierce smile that did not reach the eyes, spelling trouble for him. Slowly and carefully, making sure to keep her eyes fixed on the intruders, she pulled out an arrow.

Marian nocked the arrow aimed at the outlaw, looking straight at him through the line of the arrow. He was not smiling anymore. He whistled once, still holding her gaze, but more warily now. *He must be the leader.* The others stopped, confused at first, looking to him for guidance. Then they followed his gaze to Marian. Nobody moved and for a moment Marian felt slightly embarrassed with everyone looking at her. She had never liked much attention, but this was no time to drop the façade. Marian did not know if she was capable of killing but if she just scared them a little, perhaps she would not have to harm them. There was no way they could reach her, though they could certainly throw whatever concealed weapons they had at her. That was a risk she was willing to take.

Marian pulled her bow back until she felt the end of the arrow scratch her cheek lightly. She inhaled slowly, focusing her energy, and as she released her breath, she released the string of her bow, and the arrow landed before he had a chance to move, right between his feet. For a moment, everything was still, the men staring at her in awe. She felt a laugh bubbling inside her but refused to look silly. She had them.

All the men were ready to leave, looking to their leader for permission, but he only narrowed his eyes at her. Before she had a chance to react, he had reached for a dagger concealed within his clothes and threw it at her. She just about managed to move in time that it grazed past her arm. If she had not moved, she would be dead by now. Her arm stung but she ignored the pain. She felt alive, every part of her body thrumming in anticipation.

By instinct, Marian drew another arrow, placed it in the bow, pulled back and released. She had put so much energy into it, she could hear the arrow whiz through the air and hit him, slicing through his arm. Marian felt sick to the stomach as the arrow protruded through his arm and lodged in place. She drew another arrow, ready to spill more blood. The leader's eyes widened in shock for a split second before he snapped out of it. He pulled the arrow out of his arm, screaming in rage and agony, and ran without even a glace back to his men. The others followed quickly and Marian listened until all was peaceful once more.

Marian leaned back against the wall, sighing in relief.

"And good riddance!" Beatrice shouted, slamming the door with an almighty thud.

Marian's ears were ringing, the adrenaline coursing through her still. She watched Beatrice start to put the furniture back in its rightful place, back to her usual self. The events of the morning started to sink in, and she felt a little bit of Robin Hood slip away from her.

That dream in her mind's eye of the freedom of an outlaw started to fade. What had she been thinking? She would not rob someone's home. Robin Hood had made it seem like being an outlaw was the most liberating thing in the world, but in reality, they were murderers and thieves, forced into the forest for breaking laws. They were not good people. Suddenly Marian felt a pang of anger, not at them, but at herself for believing in such nonsense as a perfect life. It just did not exist.

"Look what they did to you," Beatrice said. Marian had been so lost in thought she did not even realise Beatrice had finished with resetting the room and was now touching her arm. She felt a sting and withdrew from Beatrice's clammy hand. She looked down at her arm, and she had forgotten the man had thrown a dagger at her. There was a line of blood around the top of her arm.

"Marian, are you alright?" A small voice came from downstairs. Marian noticed Alice stood in the corner awkwardly, not knowing what to do.

"Nothing to worry about Alice, just a scratch. You can go back to your room if you want," Marian replied. She felt sorry for Alice. Whatever had gone on in her life, it must have been quite bad. She was a nervous wreck most of the time, hidden away in the servants' quarters.

"No. I would like to start being more helpful to you. Will you give me some jobs to do?"

"Of course. I am sure Beatrice has a few things you could help her with." Marian felt cruel for never asking Alice what she wanted. She had probably come here wanting a distraction, but they had given her time to think things over instead. Marian could not escape her past quick enough, always keeping busy. Why had she been so ignorant, making Alice relive her memories.

"I will be right down with you, my love. Could you give the furniture a clean for me? I want rid of those dirty man smells all over the place. I am just going to fix Marian's arm up and I will help."

"We have been no help to her," Marian whispered.

"We gave her a home, now she needs to help herself. You forget she is only a little younger than you. You treat her like a child."

"You should have told me!"

"I know you do not like being told what to do."

"You know me too well. I would not have listened."

"Right, now none of your deeds today. You are on bed rest. Walter will not be happy if you bleed out and die."

"Cheerful as always," Marian replied. The adrenaline had worn off completely now, and her arm was throbbing in protest.

#

Walter slumped at his desk. He was in his bed chamber, the only place where he could be alone, where he did not have to be strong. The uncomfortable, wooden chair dug into his back, but he refused to move to a more comfortable position. Every day that King Richard was away fighting, the threat of Prince John and Longchamp increased.

Walter had once met the King, just before he had left for the Third Crusade. He had asked Walter to help Nottingham prosper, as one day it would be the centre of England. He would never give up on Nottingham and he would never break this promise. But he felt so trapped and utterly alone in the fight against the two opposing forces that threatened to rip England apart. And now, in front of him, was the letter he had hoped would never arrive. The King's seal was prominent, but Walter knew it was not from the King. Next to the seal was a 'J' symbolising the letter was from 'King John', as he preferred to be known as.

The Sheriff of Nottingham,

It is with great sacrifice that I must burden the magnificent city of Nottingham with an increase in taxes. You are to send me double taxes for the foreseeable future as King Richard demands it. Our soldiers are suffering and need replenishment in the fight against Saladin, Sultan of Egypt. I am certain the people will be generous and understanding as it will directly impact the swiftness of the soldiers' return.

This is not a request, but an order, and there will be severe consequences if you attempt in any way to bypass my orders. It is your job to get the people to pay, by force or otherwise.

Your future King,

Prince John

The letter made Walter want to give up, but he knew he could never do that. He could not leave the people to a worse fate. The prince was selfish and wanted to sponge off the poor to become more powerful and wealthy than he already was. Walter believed Prince John was simply feeding lies to make him more cooperative. He feared the prince knew of his unwavering loyalty to King Richard and these lies were only proof that the prince did indeed know Walter's alliance.

Prince John was, however, the lesser of two evils. Longchamp was in charge of England by the King's orders and Longchamp was, in his way, loyal to the King. But he wanted more power and Prince John was the one person stopping him from gaining all the power England had to offer. Longchamp was not a nice man to the English. He cared only for Normans and brought many of his foreign allies to England to give himself more power.

Walter was not alone in his fight against Longchamp, and he did not want to get the wrath of Prince John, so he lied that his allegiance was to him, not to the King. The only person Walter trusted was the King and he would pretend otherwise until his return, if that is what he had to do to protect Nottingham and Marian.

Walter had been named the High Sheriff of Nottinghamshire, Derbyshire and the Royal Forests by King Henry II in 1184. He had been on his way to take up his new role in Nottingham Castle when he had come across a young Marian and offered to take her in. He had never had a family, and this was his miracle from God. He vowed to God that he would give her everything she wanted and would treat her like his own daughter.

However, it had become increasingly hard to think about Marian when every day he felt frailer and more useless. He did not know whether it be due to his health declining or the stress of the job, perhaps both. He was no longer a young man and he needed no reminder of that fact. Most nights he could not sleep, thinking too much about what may happen to the people but also to Marian if he were to die. It was not a pleasant thought, but Marian was the only person he truly trusted, and though she had originally needed him, now he needed her more than ever. She was the only person he could talk openly to and he did not know how she would support herself without him in the future. She had no one but her maids, and no money but what he gave her. He had provided her with a home, supplies and weapons. What would she do without him? Deep down he knew she was more than capable of looking after herself, but she was his daughter, and to him she was still the scared little girl he found in the forest. To this day, he had not known how she had gotten those wounds on her back. If ever he were to find out who did such an unthinkable thing, he would travel to the ends of the Earth to do worse damage to them.

Chapter 3

Marian stood outside Walter's bed chambers. She knew he would be angry and overprotective about the attack on her home, and she had managed to avoid him finding out until now, but it wasn't fair on him if she didn't say anything. Marian hated hiding things from him.

Walter was often threatened by other powerful figures of authority, mainly due to the fact that his role as High Sheriff had never been officially announced or guaranteed by King Henry II. He had been appointed as second in command to the true High Sheriff, Radulf Murdac, who had been too unwell to lead. Radulf based himself in Bolsover Castle in Derbyshire, while Marian and Walter had taken up residence in Nottingham. Radulf died five years ago and since then nobody had been officially given the title, but Walter took it upon himself to ensure Nottingham was well looked after. Everyone accepted him as the High Sheriff, but Walter had always warned Marian that someone would eventually take over from him. She reassured him that he was doing a great job and the town was prospering, but it played heavily on his mind and she could do nothing to stop his anxiety.

She knocked, but was too uneasy to wait, so opened the door and peered around.

Walter was hunched over his desk but immediately looked up as she walked in.

"Marian? You look… has something happened?"

"You look a little brighter today." She smiled, using his own trick of changing the conversation.

"Do not turn this around to me. What is it?" He looked so pale, Marian did not want to make things worse.

"We have a problem with outlaws. Or at least we did until I sorted them out." Marian could tell by the shock on his face that she should not have told him. The last thing he needed was to worry more about her. She knew now that no matter what she told him, he would not be happy that she put herself in danger. He, like everyone else, believed a woman should not be skilled in such disciplines as fighting. It had taken time to sway him into letting her, but he had eventually given up when she would not back down. She had told him it was only to defend herself, but it was more than that.

"What in God's name happened?!" He stood and took her arm before she could pull it away. He carefully unwrapped the bandage.

"It is just a scratch. Trust me; I dealt them a lot more damage." She smiled proudly.

"Them? How many *were* there?!"

"Only six or seven. Anyway, they were not very well equipped to fight. I guess they targeted my home because I am a *woman*." Marian narrowed her eyes at Walter judgingly; she knew he held the same belief, though he had never said as much.

"I cannot believe how reckless you are!" He stood, anger blushing his cheeks.

"What did you expect? That I would just hide until it was over? They were not nice people, and if they had found me, what do you think they might have done to me? Or if I had not have stopped them, they might have harmed my maids. I had to do something!"

Walter returned to his desk defeated. She knew he would act like this, but he did not know what she was capable of.

"What did you do to them?" he asked.

"I warned them off, that is all." It was much more than that, but she did not want to burden him with the details. He would be outraged.

"I will send my guards to search for any trace of them. I am giving you two of my guards to protect your home. I do not want you fighting like a soldier. I need to know you are safe."

Marian scowled at the thought of others protecting her. "I am sure they will not return. They must be far away by now. They will not want more arrows embedded in them.

"And do *not* send any guards my way or I will deal with them myself." Marian stormed out.

#

Walter had once told Marian of a secret chamber behind the hall where local meetings took place. She did not want to ask Walter what was causing him so much distress so she decided to listen in, purely out of curiosity. She had always admired Walter's openness about the secret room just behind the Sheriff's chair. He had told her about it when she enquired about what men talk about, striving to be on the same level as a man, intellectually.

Marian made her way to the secret room during the guard change over to make sure no one would see her. Although Walter had told her about the room and the guards knew of its existence in case of an emergency, no one knew Marian had been told about it, and she wanted to keep it that way.

Marian found the small ledge and pulled it open, just enough to squeeze inside, and shut it, making sure not to make a noise. The room was more the size of a wardrobe; she filled the width of it, sitting down with her knees hugged to her chest. There was no meeting due on today, so she closed her eyes and tried to clear her mind. It was so quiet here compared to the rest of the castle. It seemed a million miles away from reality, just how she liked it. There was nothing to remind her of anything, and usually she would be able to sit still and listen to the sound of silence, allowing her to be herself without fear of judgment.

But this time, there was too much on her mind. Walter's face kept appearing whenever she closed her eyes; he looked so pale and tired. She could not help but worry. She fidgeted and could not relax, her shoulders aching from tension. After a few minutes, she could no longer stand it; there was simply too much going on in her mind. Suddenly the hall doors opened and several nobles entered the room. She made herself comfortable and peered through the slit in the wall in front of her.

Walter never called last minute meetings, especially on market day when the nobles were all busy. Something must be wrong. The nobles were dressed in their usual attire, wearing their finest clothes to prove their wealth and power to the world. They were not like Walter; they were selfish and uncaring of others. Finally, Walter entered and sat on his chair, his back to Marian.

"My lords, I thank you for your presence here today. As you may have guessed, this is not our usual weekly meeting. We have a serious matter to attend to." Walter's voice was careful but urgent. Marian watched, her heart racing. "I received a letter today from Prince John. He has asked... no, ordered Nottingham's taxes to be doubled." Whispers of shock radiated around the hall. Marian could not even imagine what that would do to the people. She had heard of their troubles from her maids. The people were barely surviving paying the taxes at the current rate. Doubling the taxes would cripple Nottingham, there was no way they could raise that much money.

The doors opened once more and the room fell silent. Marian tried to reposition herself to see who had entered, but all the nobles had gotten to their feet and she could not see around them.

"I apologise for my lateness. Please continue." Marian had not noticed before but there was a spare seat when the nobles sat back down. She could now see the man. He was tall, and his clothes were unlike those of the others. He wore all black, an almost armour-like material. She looked at his face to see if she could recognise him, and he was looking straight back at her. She cringed away from the gap in the wood. Surely, he could not see her? He looked away, walked to his chair and sat down. He nodded at Walter to continue.

"This is..." Walter stumbled for words. He seemed on edge and taken aback.

"Sir Guy of Gisbourne. I have been appointed to... *support* Nottingham. You were expecting me, Walter. Do you recall?" He spoke down to Walter as though he were above the Sheriff. Marian wanted to tell him to show some respect but she could not give away that she was listening in. All she knew was that she did not like this intruder. He spelled trouble, and she could sense it. Walter did not answer. "I will be leading your troops in their efforts against law breakers such as those who do not pay their taxes. Prince John is assured that you will abide by the tax increase to help King Richard in his crusade. I am your appointed Constable." He spoke like a strict leader. It seemed, Marian suspected, that Guy of Gisbourne had been sent personally by Prince John to do his dirty work. Her stomach turned at the thought. She could tell, that if Walter even put a foot wrong, this man would not hesitate to report it to Prince John.

"I was not expecting you until at least tomorrow. How did you arrive so quickly?"

"I followed close behind the messenger. I felt I needed to be here sooner rather than later. Once the tax increase comes into operation tomorrow, I expect some will refuse. Let me make this clear." Marian watched as Guy of Gisbourne stood, marched over to Walter and stood in front of him addressing the nobles. "If anyone should refuse to pay, the consequences shall be severe. Implemented immediately, I am to have full control over the soldiers." No one dared to speak or protest. Marian watched, praying someone would stand up to him, but she knew deep down that they would not go against Prince John's orders. Guy of

Gisbourne meant business. There was nothing they could do to improve the situation. He looked around at each noble slowly, watching to see if they would speak up. No one did. He turned around and gave a stern look to Walter. Walter had been undermined and could do nothing to stop Guy of Gisbourne.

"Meeting adjourned." Guy of Gisbourne waited as each lord left silently, and finally Walter stood and trailed out, all strength gone. He did not even raise his head, and Marian could see his life force draining even faster than it had been.

Gisbourne did not deserve any title or rank, so she would not give him one. He was a rodent, nothing more. He let the doors close behind Walter and stood still for a moment. She watched him suspiciously. He started walking around the hall very slowly, examining every wall closely. *How could he know about the hidden room?* As that thought passed her mind, she realised he was coming towards her. Marian clambered to get out. She just managed to sneak out unnoticed before she heard a creak. She was certain Gisbourne had found her hiding spot. With her nerves beaten, she had to get away. She could not bear to meet this mysterious, deadly stranger when she had not yet gotten her head around what she had just witnessed, and what it meant for Nottingham.

Chapter 4

"Let this be an example to you all!" Gisbourne boomed across the square. Beatrice had followed him all morning on Marian's request. She was shocked to see the people being treated with such malice and cruelty, and Gisbourne's temper was getting worse as the day wore on.

She stared in disbelief as he physically dragged a woman by her hair across the gravel.

"You will pay or you will face my wrath!" This was all a show to Gisbourne. Beatrice could see this was what his superiors wanted – terror. She had watched people hand over their last valuables to avoid his rage.

She followed Gisbourne to the poorest district, and he knocked on the door of a small, tired home. When no one answered, he kicked the door down and stormed inside. Beatrice could hear shouts and screams that made her blood boil. He had no right to barge in and demand money; it was unjust. Gisbourne reappeared with several guards who had followed him inside. They were pushing the family outside for the public to see. A slim, malnourished woman shook with fear while her husband started towards their three children, one of which looked only just old enough to walk. Gisbourne forced the father back.

"Where is the money?" Gisbourne demanded. A crowd was starting to form around the scene but none dared to get too close.

"I…" the father began, ready to protest, but then seemed to give up. "Here," he handed over a few meagre coins. "It is all we have to survive on." Beatrice's heart sank. She could not believe what she was witnessing. Gisbourne tossed the coins in his hand and looked at the father with dangerous eyes.

"The King requires more than this." He turned to his guards. "Find anything of value and bring it to me."

"I sold the last few items of worth to pay my taxes last month. We have nothing left," the father pleaded.

"I am unlike your fragile Sheriff. Such lenience is a sign of weakness. Do I look like a weak man to you? Prince John has given me the authority to use any means necessary." He turned to the crowd around him. "Let this be a lesson to you all. It is your duty to pay your taxes. If you do not, you are a criminal in the eyes of the law and you will be treated as such." He turned to a guard and nodded. The guard approached the father and held his sword. He escorted the father to a log and placed his hand against it. The father started to squirm fearfully, and more guards approached, holding him in place. Beatrice turned away, unable to watch as the crowd gasped. Her blood ran cold, knowing without having to look, that he had lost a hand just for being poor. There was a big possibility he would not survive – nobody in the poor quarter could afford a physician. Gisbourne did not seem the type to care either way.

#

Marian was practicing her knife throwing into a tree when Beatrice returned from her errand. By the look on Beatrice's face, it was even worse than she had thought. After Beatrice had divulged the gruesome details, Marian could not sit idly by and let it continue. But first she needed more information, and she knew exactly who could help her.

Friar Tuck used to be a godly man of the church, visiting towns around England, preaching to the people. He had come to Nottingham on his travels and decided to stay, living in St. Mary's Church, close to Marian's manor. Marian lived just a few streets south of the church, passing it whenever she ventured out. In her first year in Nottingham, she had approached Tuck in search of a way to make sense of her life and the pain her uncle had put her through. Tuck had advised her to find a way to feel safe once more, which was what had originally sparked her desire to be able to protect herself from others. After a while though, he started to change. He had taken up drinking and lost sight of God. As Marian gained a purpose, Tuck had lost his.

Marian had never been a religious person, but she believed in fate. She still visited Tuck from time to time. He was easy to find, always outside the inn, hoping to get a free drink or two. Tuck could not resist a good gossip and people paid him well to find information. On occasion Walter had even hired him to keep an eye on certain regulars.

Marian walked to the inn alone. She was not very recognisable, infamously a recluse to the townspeople. It worked in her favour as no one ever questioned who she was, and she was able to avoid any unwanted attention. Walter provided her with clothes and he always insisted she wear feminine gowns of nobility, but she preferred to dress down to blend in when she ventured out. Now she wore a simple white dress with a cloak to keep out the chill of late Spring. She wandered along the smaller streets. It took longer this way, but it was a more relaxing walk than the large crowds of the main street leading to the inn.

When she arrived, she was surprised to find that Tuck was not in his usual spot outside. She lifted the hood on her cloak closer to her face, relieved of the protection it provided in a place where men preyed on women. She did not even dare to think of the dreadful things that happened inside.

Just as she suspected, Tuck was sat at a corner table clutching an ale as though it might sprout legs and run. He was staring intently at the ale in his hands, but Marian could tell he was concentrating on something else. She sat next to him quietly and waited. She had seen him like this before. Eventually he gave a nod in the direction that he was listening so she could focus her attention on it as well. And there he was.

Gisbourne sat in the centre of the room, near the bar, a busy crowded area. He obviously did not want to be recognised either, for he had his head down, whispering to a woman. She wore simple, worn clothes, and her fingers gripped an apron folded in her lap. Marian recognised her from the castle as one of the kitchen maids. The fact that Gisbourne was talking to a servant was not a good thing. Marian suspected he was not the sort of man to talk to anyone of a low rank other than to give demands. Gisbourne gave the maid a small pouch and she walked off, hiding it under her apron.

Marian leant over to Tuck and whispered thanks before placing a little money on the table for him. Gisbourne left promptly and Marian followed, making sure to keep her distance so as not to arouse suspicion. She followed him out of the inn and down several streets. He turned a corner and she waited for a few moments before following. This was leading further away from the castle, and she grew even more suspicious that, although he had full control of the guards, there were none in sight. Gisbourne continued swerving down the busy streets and towards the market square.

It was Saturday and the market was busier than usual, with more stalls than Marian had ever seen before. She did not doubt they were trying to get any extra money they could to pay the taxes, their fear of Gisbourne driving them to extremes to avoid his wrath. What disturbed Marian the most was that there were hardly any buyers.

Marian looked around frantically. She had become distracted by the sorry state of the market, and lost Gisbourne. He could have gone down any number of streets off of the market square. After a few minutes of searching, she gave up and started to head home before darkness fell.

On her way back, Marian noticed someone lurking around the corner from her home. She decided to confront him, to find out what he was doing. People rarely walked close to her home and she wanted to keep it that way.

"Are you lost? Can I help you?" she tried to disguise the formality of her voice to come across as a peasant.

"Me? I am not lost. I was just admiring that manor."

"Well if you were thinking of taking up residency there, I would have to warn you against it."

"Why is that?" He looked at her judgingly. She wondered whether he might be another thief, ready to ransack her home.

"The recluse lives there. She, well... I have heard she is not the nicest of people. I would not want to get on her bad side." Just to add to the drama, she whispered, "everyone thinks she is crazy." It was fun for Marian to tell such stories.

"I like a good challenge!" Not the response she expected. He continued admiring her home. She did not know what to make of him.

"So, why are you lurking around here? Planning on killing the witch and taking the manor for yourself?"

"What witch?"

"But of course, the witch who lives inside. They say if you kill her, you will be cursed forever." Marian enjoyed her little game, but she found it hard to keep a straight face.

"Alright, stop with the stories! I am guessing you live in that place?"

"Why would you think that?" Marian replied too protectively, suddenly wary of this stranger's motives.

"It is what I would do if I wanted to be left alone. I am sorry if I worried you then. It is just... I am looking for work, and I thought maybe the person living there could offer me some. I did try with the other maids, but they would not even let me see the owner."

"Sorry. I do not know if she is looking for servants at the moment. Perhaps if I knew a little about you, I could put in a good word."

"Did you say a woman owns this home, on her own?" he said, astonished. She knew men's opinions of a woman's place well. Even Walter had been reluctant to let her live there without a male presence in the household. It was extremely rare for a woman to live alone.

"Yes. Is that so bad?"

"No. Well, ah. Yes. You see I have a… difficult past and I do not think I am very employable. I have worked at many different jobs in the past and I can learn. I would be happy to do anything that is required of me."

"Alright, what are your skills?"

"I come from a family of blacksmiths. I know how to craft weapons, though I cannot see any use a woman would have for those. Like I said, I am happy to learn." Marian was suspicious as to why he had decided to say about the blacksmith background. She worried he might be lying, perhaps having heard that she was a skilled fighter. Who was he working for?

"Have you heard of Sir Guy of Gisbourne?" she asked, on a whim.

"Why do you ask?" his shoulders tightened instantly; Marian sensed she had touched a nerve.

"So, you know him?"

"I have heard of him. I met him once. How do you know him? He lives a long way from here."

"No. He lives here, in the castle. He moved in a few days ago."

"Here? But how… how did he find us?" He was talking too quickly. He knew things about Gisbourne, and she needed to know.

"Us? What are you talking about?" He looked distant and ready to leave.

"I cannot tell you. Do not bother telling the owner. I need to go." He started to walk away, hurriedly. He was no friend of Gisbourne. Perhaps he could be an ally. She would have to reveal a piece of herself to earn his trust.

"Wait," Marian pleaded. "I am no friend of Gisbourne either. If you want a job, prove it to me. I am the owner of this manor. Please come in and tell me what you know about Gisbourne."

Chapter 5

Beatrice huffed at Marian. "I sense nothing good will come of this. I do not trust him. How did he find this place? He is not from around here, that much is certain. Please, Marian, send him on his way. Does Walter know that you are putting yourself in danger?"

"Do not bring Walter into this. He does not need to know anything. This man knows of Gisbourne, and they are certainly not friends. That is all I need to know. We will give him a chance. Just one chance."

"You are too stubborn for your own good! Watch your back. I will not always be there to watch it for you."

"Please keep yourself busy for a while, I want him to feel at ease, not with your glaring eyes following him." At that, Beatrice turned her back and stormed off. Marian turned her attention to the young man, sat uncomfortably on the edge of a chair. She watched him reposition himself a few times, like he had never sat on a chair before.

"Please relax. You are in no danger here. My name is Marian, I am Sheriff Walter's daughter. I am no friend of Gisbourne. He is reigning terror on the people of Nottingham, and it needs to stop. Could you tell me what you know of him? Do not worry, Gisbourne does not know me, he will not come here." He eased a little but did not speak. "What is your name?"

"Jack. I am new around here, though I would not have come if I knew he would be here. I am useful, Lady. My parents were blacksmiths, and I learnt a lot from them. I am a fast learner and I can fight as well. Although I do not think a lady such as yourself gets much trouble."

"You would be surprised, Jack. How did you end up here? Your accent is not familiar." Marian was starting to like him, he seemed genuine.

"I come from the south. I had to leave my family. You see, a new blacksmith set up near us. They were richer, and had better equipment, so our customers went to them instead. We lost our trade and our money. The bailiff had an arrest

31

warrant for us, as we had nothing left to pay the taxes. My parents told me to run, and I did. I never looked back. I heard a few days later in a nearby village that my parents had resisted arrest and been killed."

"I am so sorry. Powerful men do not see people, they only see money and opportunity. We have seen our share of injustice here as well. I am not sure this is a good place for you to settle, especially with Gisbourne."

"But it is. I have never met Gisbourne, only heard stories that would be too cruel to speak of to a Lady. You see, I was an outlaw for a time. I had no money to start again, so went to the forest. If it weren't for a gang of outlaws, I would probably be dead now. The outlaws were on the run from a man named Gisbourne. He was close to Prince John and had a lot of man power at his disposal to hunt down criminals like ourselves. I did not stay in the gang for long. This is the first place I came across. I heard about this manor, the people stay away from it. Please, Lady, I just need to keep my head down and get away from prying eyes. I understand if you do not want an unworthy criminal in your home and I will leave without question if you wish it. I just want to learn to be a good person again."

Marian sat back in her chair. She trusted Jack enough to let him into her home and even though he was an outlaw, he just wanted a second chance at life. Walter had given her a chance. Perhaps this was her new calling. She also had a curiosity for outlaws and it stirred up memories of Robin Hood, the boy who almost saved her. Marian had to give Jack this chance. It simply felt like the right thing to do. It was a big step in the right direction for her to start trusting people again.

"I will give you a room in the servants' quarters. You start tomorrow."

#

It turned out Jack was indeed a very hard worker and Marian believed she had made a good decision. She had been at first nervous that her foremost real responsibility would be a mistake. But Jack did not ask questions or pry; he simply got on with his job and stayed out of everyone's way. It had only been two days but Marian trusted Jack and was proud of herself for giving him a chance. She invited him to start training with her and he even offered to make her arrows, rather than going through Walter to supply them. She was pleased to have a new friend at home and enjoyed the company.

A week later, Marian was getting ready for bed, watching the sky darken from the window in her chambers.

"Marian!" Jack called up. The first thing she had asked of him was to stop calling her a Lady. "You have a visitor," he continued when she did not answer. She never had visitors. Maybe it was Walter checking in on her, but at this hour? Her maids had not yet been up to dress her in her night clothes, so she walked downstairs, only to see Gisbourne in her home.

He was sat on the bench by the fireplace. As she walked past Jack, she squeezed his arm as a hint to stay in the room.

Gisbourne did not acknowledge Marian as she approached him from behind. She had no clue how he even knew where she lived, let alone why he was here. They had not been formally introduced, which only unsettled her more.

He sat very upright, the position of a man who believed himself to be of very high importance. It made her stomach churn as his obnoxious demeanour reminded her of her uncle. Marian had intentionally avoided Gisbourne, and she only knew who he was because she had listened in on the Sheriff's meeting. He could not possibly know her, could he? Perhaps he had found out she was spying on him. She breathed deeply, trying to calm her nerves. It did not work.

"Excuse me for seeming rude, but who are you and what are you doing in my home?" Marian asked in a sharp manner, to let him know exactly who he was toying with. At that moment, Gisbourne turned his head to look at her. At first, his face was alarmingly concentrated and still, but it changed as soon as his eyes settled on her hands.

"I see you are unmarried," was all he said. Marian hid her hands behind her back and felt her cheeks blush. Walter had allowed her to choose who she would marry. He would never force a betrothal. Was this why Gisbourne had come to her? He would certainly not have heard this information from Walter. Then, who?

She had never thought about marriage before. All she knew was that she would never marry this *animal* before her. She looked to Gisbourne and suddenly felt very aware of herself, his stare making her feel exposed and nervous. Was this his intention? To marry her? She still did not understand how he even knew her, and he was avoiding answering her questions. Defensively, Marian crossed her arms, opened her mouth and asked once more.

"Do you care to answer me? If not, you may leave."

He held his position for a moment, and then adopted a more formal attitude.

"I apologise for my rudeness. My name is Sir Guy of Gisbourne." *Too much emphasis on the 'sir'*, Marian thought. "I heard the Sheriff speak of you in such high regard, I thought I should see for myself. It was such a contradiction of the locals' opinions, though they *are* savages." Just as she expected; lies. But what was he hiding?

She would not get the answers she wanted out of him. Walter never talked much about her to anyone. It had been her own request and she trusted Walter to keep his promise. It had taken him a while but he had come to respect her wishes without question. If people knew her as insane, they would leave her alone. Originally, Walter had backed her up every time a bad rumour spread, but eventually he let it go, when he realised her reasons.

"How noble of you." She did not mean for it to sound so patronising, but she could not stand his arrogance. He raised an eyebrow, realising Marian could stand up for herself. She laughed inwardly at this thought, but she did not dare make it obvious to him – he seemed dangerous, not a person to cross. Gisbourne appeared to be a man who would want an obedient wife, and he could not have chosen a more opposing character if he tried. He sat for a moment longer, assessing the situation in front of him. *He must be of a high position*, Marian thought, *as not many men actually analyse before running into a situation full steam ahead.* Most men, Marian believed, did not have the capacity to be so clever as to think before they act. Gisbourne seemed more calculating than most men.

Marian took Gisbourne's pause as an opportunity to glance over at Jack, still stood in the corner of the room by the stairway. Jack shifted his eye line to two guards posted at the open door. Marian had not noticed them before; they must have snuck in when she was observing Gisbourne. The moment ended and Gisbourne stood abruptly. He was very tall and overpowered Marian in every way. He was broad and muscular, while Marian was of an average shape, though she had a good appetite so her muscles had a thin layer of fat covering them. She did not look much of a fighter, which worked to her advantage.

Gisbourne waved a guard over and Marian was instantly apprehensive. She held her position, refusing to back down, but mentally prepared herself for attack. The guard handed a box to Gisbourne and returned to his station. Marian relaxed a little.

"Perhaps you require something to show you how *giving* I can be." Marian felt sick to the stomach. She needed to show him that nothing could make her want him. She would not marry this man, she promised herself. She knew she was not the most desirable woman but surely, she could do better than him? And if not, she would be more than happy to stay single the rest of her life than marry this beast. He opened the box, and inside was a beautiful necklace, worth more than Marian could imagine. She loved to dress up when the need arose, in the expensive clothes Walter always provided her with, but she rarely had an occasion to match. She deemed jewellery useless, it was beautiful but there was no purpose to it, apart from to show wealth. She believed the only jewellery that should be worn would be for sentimentality, like the ring her mother had given to her before she died, which hung on a chain around her neck. Even though it was probably not worth a lot of money, to her it was worth the world. It reminded her that her mother was always there with her.

Marian tried to turn him down politely, uncertain of how he might react. He looked like a man who always got what he wanted.

"A generous gift, but I cannot accept it..." Before she could continue, she paused, taken aback. His expression changed instantly, and she could sense she had done the wrong thing. He suddenly threw the necklace on the floor, the box clanging loudly as it hit the ground, sending a thrum through her ears. Gisbourne grabbed her wrists before she could pull away.

"You *dare* refuse a gift from me?! Do you know who I am, little girl?" Marian felt naked, with his eyes looking at her as though she were a piece of meat ready to be eaten. His grip on her wrists was so tight her hands started to lose feeling and her wrists throbbed painfully. And then Jack was beside her.

"I am sure she only means for you to prove your affection towards her in another manner than gifts."

"And what would you recommend I do?" he said through gritted teeth, making no effort to loosen his grip.

"A gesture to win her heart," Jack suggested. His voice was a welcome steadiness through the chaos in her mind.

Gisbourne considered this for a moment, and finally let Marian go. "Very well, I accept the challenge. I shall see you shortly, my Lady." At that he stormed out. In his mind, Marian guessed, he had already won. He pushed his guards out the way and they followed him.

Beatrice appeared from the servants' quarters and Marian watched in silence as she closed the door. Jack walked over and tried to look at her wrists, but she stepped back from him. She just wanted to be alone.

"Thank you for your help. I am in your debt." Marian turned to Beatrice who was trying to make sense of what had just happened. "Beatrice, I am retiring to my bed chamber."

Marian ignored the bruises on her wrists and tried to will away the pain. It was not too painful but she knew it would be worse in the morning. She tiresomely walked up the stairs, trying desperately to act normal. Beatrice was hot on her heels, ready to change Marian into her nightdress for bed as usual. Beatrice made no attempt to question Marian, knowing full well Marian would not answer anyway.

Chapter 6

Alan a Dale's heart raced uncomfortably as he followed the forest path to Arthur a Bland. He was terrified of this man; a dangerous predator of an outlaw. He feared more so for what would happen if he did not show up. Alan had told Marian the truth but left out a few key points. One being that he was still an outlaw – in the worst gang possible. Arthur a Bland had been part of Alan's old gang, having been close to the leader. However, unknown to the leader, Arthur was going behind his back, recruiting for his own gang.

A few days ago, Arthur had returned from a raid worn and injured. Alan had not long become a part of his rogue gang and Arthur had not yet trusted him, leaving him to tend to camp while they went to work. When they had returned, Arthur had marched over to him and barked orders.

"Alan. You will go to Nottingham, to a manor with a horrid woman. You will become her friend, you will find her weaknesses and you will report back to me in seven days at sundown." He had not questioned Arthur, knowing full well the man had a bad temper. Alan had left immediately, relieved to get away from camp for a while.

Now he was in a sticky situation. He had expected it to be an easy task, but Marian was his friend and he could not betray her.

Alan had not always been such a rogue. Until a few weeks ago, he had been part of the original gang of outlaws who had saved him in the forest. The old leader died just over a year ago and his son had taken up the position. This new leader had rules and rarely let them pursue any big raids. Most of their days consisted of waiting around and hoping a trader would venture through their forest. It was a slow business with limited rewards.

Arthur had promised riches and gold if outlaws sided with him instead. All their leader knew was that Arthur was running errands and needed some of his men to help. Arthur had offered an exciting life rather than the boredom Alan had recently been faced with. However, Alan now realised Arthur had no care for the lives of his men. He felt a pang of guilt towards his leader. He had been right all along; it was best to stick to forest finds, not just for safety, but it was also better for your soul. Invading people's homes was just too far for Alan; home is the one place you should feel safe. A few of the men could still remember having a place they could call home, some with families that they had to leave behind or… who died.

From the start, Alan had not wanted to lie to Marian. He had told the truth about wanting to start afresh. He was disillusioned by life in the forest and wanted a real life where he could earn an honest living. Arthur was cruel, but Alan would not just give Marian to him. She was his friend; they had an understanding and she was kind to him. If only to clear his conscience, he needed to come clean to Marian. She would know what to do. Under her guidance, he could see himself learning new crafts and becoming a decent man once more. He could see her strength and felt a desire to protect her, even though he knew she could protect herself. But first he had to meet with Arthur to avoid suspicion.

Alan did not want to leave Marian, just after she had endured Gisbourne, who he knew to be very harsh and controlling. He had heard stories from the other outlaws of the feud between them and Gisbourne. Various rumours circulated around camp from time to time, but he could never figure out the truth. All he knew was that Gisbourne had been hunting them for a long time, even killing one of their own.

Alan had once caught a glimpse of Gisbourne, but at Marian's tonight he had seen him up close for the first time. The rumours of his ruthlessness were true. Alan was worried about leaving Marian alone after such a confrontation and he wished he had stepped in sooner, before Gisbourne had hurt her. Marian had not even let him see the bruises on her wrists but as she had walked up the stairs, he had seen the raw, purpling skin and wondered how she could be so resigned about such a thing. He could tell she certainly did not trust men, and he did not blame her, but he could not help but wonder how she had become that way.

What had made her so untrusting in the first place?

For a moment, Alan contemplated not showing up to report to Arthur, but that would only put Marian in more danger. He was betraying her but he would find a way out. Now that Gisbourne was in Nottingham perhaps that would refocus Arthur away from Marian. Once he was certain the maids were asleep, he had snuck out.

It was hard for Alan to reach the meeting point after dark without any source of light, but he did not want to attract any unwanted attention. He had memorised the route to Marian's from Arthur's description, but reversing it in the dark took a lot longer. He was not the brightest spark, but he thought he could at least outsmart Arthur, who relied on actions alone.

After an exhausting walk, he finally reached the clearing in the forest where the rogues frequently met. He waited for a few minutes in silent darkness. The clearing was large and vulnerable, so he stayed at the side, trying to hide from view. Much of Sherwood Forest was open, compared to most of the other forests they ventured into, which were covered in dense woodland. It gave them space, but it was also more dangerous, as there were less places to hide and ambushes were easier.

The outlaws feared Arthur; he did not look like much, but he was mysterious and dangerous. Nobody knew very much about him. Their leader was the only one who seemed to be able to freely talk to him with no fear, though he did not know Arthur was rebelling.

Alan longed for the security of his old gang once more. He felt constantly on edge around Arthur, like he could explode at any moment, taking them all down with him.

Simultaneously, Arthur and his followers appeared in the clearing. There seemed to be more than before and there were even a few he did not recognise. New outlaws always sought protection from anyone who was willing to offer it, no matter how shady the character. The forest was a dangerous place to be alone. Arthur approached him, and the others followed suit, forming a circle around him. Alan needed to look confident; Arthur did not like weak people. His eyes gave away nothing.

"What news of that witch?" he spoke with disgust, his voice echoing. He always spoke loudly, and it made him all the more fearsome.

"I did as you said. I got close to her." He thought to distract Arthur. "There is a complication." He watched Arthur's bored expression; he was not a patient man. "Gisbourne is in Nottingham."

Arthur's eyes widened, and suddenly Alan understood. Something connected Arthur to Gisbourne; they were enemies. His expression quickly returned to normal before Alan could dissect it any further. That was the first glimpse Alan had into Arthur's life, and it only frightened him more. Alan had always thought their leader had a connection to Gisbourne, but all along it had been Arthur. He was on the run from Gisbourne. What had Arthur done for Gisbourne to dedicate his whole life to capturing him, and any other outlaw he came across?

Arthur narrowed his eyes, looking into the distance. He was impulsive and ill tempered. Alan could see his mind fighting against instincts, to try to think coherently, like a leader. He had always been too quick making decisions.

"Where is he and what is he doing in Nottingham?" he demanded. Alan felt as though he were being interrogated. He answered quickly before Arthur's temper exploded.

"I only saw him at Marian's, the witch's," he added when he realised Arthur neither knew nor cared what her name was. He seemed more vengeful towards Gisbourne than Marian now. Alan's plan was working. "He was trying to woo her. She told me he was the new captain of the guard in Nottingham. By the sound of things, he had planted himself there by permission of Prince John."

One of Arthur's men, a muscular, short fellow who Alan could not name, opened his mouth.

"What about the witch? We have to do something about her. She crossed you. She has to pay!" Arthur turned to him sharply. But then his expression softened.

"Scar, my old friend, a very good observation!" A wicked smile crept over his face. Alan swallowed, dread consuming him. He looked at Scar with distaste. They must have known each other quite well. A huge scar ran from below his left eye, down past the right side of his mouth, granting him the nickname Scar. His identity seemed as much a mystery as Arthur's. It was not uncommon for outlaws to hide their pasts, but usually a story or two would be revealed over time as everyone grew closer. These two were the exceptions. Scar had not even been seen in camp before. Alan thought he must be Arthur's secret weapon.

A dangerous smile danced across Arthur's face. Alan could not bear to think what plan he had hatched.

"Alan, you will kidnap Marian, leaving a trail behind for Gisbourne to follow. It will lead him straight here, where we will ambush and kill him. Finally! I have been waiting so long for this." Alan believed him. Arthur had never been a smart man and Alan did not want to put Marian in the middle of one of his botched plans, but he was not brave enough to stand up to him now. He decided he would tell Marian everything when he got back to her. If she threw him out, he would not blame her. He deserved no better.

"What will happen to Marian?" he asked, trying to mask his concern.

"Well, lucky for her, Gisbourne is more important. Bring her here by the sun's highest point tomorrow so Gisbourne has enough time. I am trusting you to put this plan into action.

"Do not fail me. Oh, and Alan, make sure Gisbourne gets the message."

Arthur turned and left as swiftly as he had arrived, with his rogues following closely behind, muttering and laughing between themselves. Alan's stomach lurched as he turned his back on them and started towards Nottingham. By the time he arrived back, the sun would be rising. Then he would tell Marian the truth.

Chapter 7

"My Lady, wake up!"

Marian bolted out of bed so quickly the blood rushed to her head and it took her a moment to realise Beatrice was looking at her, her hair tousled. She was in a fluster about something or other.

The room was light; she must have slept in. This seemed to be happening more often as of late. Her wrists throbbed with the unsettling memory of the previous evening with Gisbourne.

"What is it Beatrice?" She blinked, trying to fight off the grogginess that clung to her.

"It is Jack. He snuck out last night. He is back and wishes to speak with you urgently."

At that, Marian nodded, Beatrice understanding their unspoken language. Without another word, Beatrice dressed her in a loose fitting, simple dress with long sleeves to cover her bruised wrists. She did not want to be known as a victim, and she certainly did not want to be fussed over. This injury was nothing compared to what she had endured in her past, both physically and mentally.

Beatrice put Marian's hair into a quick braid, very unlike the style of the time, but Marian's purpose was comfort more than fashion. Most women still hid their hair with a wimple, which Marian thought outdated and unnecessary. It was, as with most other things, a statement of possession, that only the husband could see his woman's hair in its true form.

She rolled her eyes at the thought.

As soon as she was decent enough, Marian rushed down to see what Jack needed to discuss. After yesterday, she was indebted to him.

Marian found Jack pacing around the furniture. When he saw her approach, he stopped abruptly. He gestured nervously for Marian to sit down. She moved over to her usual chair and Jack followed, sitting on a nearby stool. She could tell he was not used to such luxuries as a comfy chair; he adjusted and fidgeted until he was comfortable. When he would not speak, it only served to make Marian more anxious.

"What is it Jack? What is wrong?" she asked impatiently.

"I need to tell you a… story. My story. The truth. I was not honest to you and I hate myself for it." Marian knew he had been hiding something but she could not blame him. She had been living behind a lie for years.

"Okay," she said cautiously. "Tell it from the start and leave nothing out. I want to know everything."

"Well, my name is Alan a Dale, most of what I told you was true, about my past anyway. I come from a family of blacksmiths in the South, one day a new blacksmith started taking business from us, and my family could not pay their taxes. I was only thirteen, and the debt collector was ruthless. My parents told me to run as guards tore down our home. I hid out of sight and watched as my parents protested and got in the way. They were killed in front of me. There was nothing I could do. I ran for the forest. I knew that if I stayed, I would be at best imprisoned, at worst hung. I did not know where I was going but I walked endlessly, trying to find somewhere to start a new life. I did not know how to look after myself, but I had been taught to defend myself with the dagger my father had made for me. I managed to survive a day but when night came, I had no shelter from the cold and winter was approaching. I huddled under some branches and I just about lasted the night.

"The next morning, starvation hit. I tried to hunt with my dagger. I knew it was illegal and punishable by death but I was already an outlaw so I thought I may as well act like one or die helpless. It turned out I could not hunt very well. I ended up by a river and managed to catch a couple of fish to survive. I still had no clue where I was or what to do with myself. I curled up for another night in the cold. I closed my eyes ready for sleep when I heard movement. A voice erupted above me. At first, I believed God was talking to me. But then I opened my eyes. A great man loomed over me. He told me I had a life ahead of me, that he had rescued many like me from the clutches of death. He said there was a life waiting for me, free of the laws of the King.

"The outlaws made me a skilled man and taught me how to survive in the forest. I became their personal blacksmith, learning new techniques of making weapons without the equipment I had been used to. The only thing they asked for in return for my safety was to help them in their thieving. I had nothing better to do with my time and at first the idea of it was exciting. I grew to enjoy being an outlaw and they became like family to me. Though when my saviour died, a younger man took over. He had been trained up to be the next leader, but he was different…"

"Sorry," Marian interrupted. "It is hard to follow without names."

"I am sorry Marian. I trust you, but I owe them my life. I cannot reveal their names. The more you know, the more danger they are in. The gang I was part of are probably the nicest group of outlaws you would ever come across. They are not perfect, but they have rules and do not rob people's homes, only those who step into their part of the forest. I will try to make it as clear as possible.

"Recently I have grown less inspired by our leader. He restricted us and watched us very closely. He brought in an old friend, Arthur a Bland. He was a dark and cruel man, from what I had heard. I believed him to be our leader's spy, to keep us all in order. However, our leader did not know that Arthur was taking outlaws to start his own gang. I recently found out Arthur is on the run from Gisbourne. Only when I met you did I realise Gisbourne was now here in Nottingham. He must have somehow tracked us here.

"At first, I thought joining Arthur was a good idea. He offered us freedom and riches. He wants revenge on you for getting in their way when they tried to rob you. He is angry that you wounded him. He told me to get close to you and expose your weaknesses. If he had any brains, he would leave you alone. I realise now I made a mistake. I should have stayed with our leader, but I am glad I have met you. You have taught me so much. I am telling you the truth now because I want to stay with you. I cannot put you in harm's way. I want to be an honest man and you are helping me become that person. I came here believing you to be an evil witch, but you are the kindest person I have ever met. I was misled and I am sorry. I went to Arthur last night to try and refocus his anger on Gisbourne rather than you, but I have only made it worse. Marian, he is a very dangerous man. If you want me to leave, I will understand. He told me to kidnap you and use you as bait to trap Gisbourne."

It took a few minutes for Marian to process everything. She had always been so careful before now. She did believe him, and she respected his honesty. He had had a tough life and made some bad choices. She could not find it in her to blame him, but she was angry at herself for letting her guard down.

"What made you tell me the truth? Why did you not just go ahead with the plan?"

"I do not want to be a part of it anymore. I am tired of lying to myself that I am doing the right thing. I know my parents would not have been proud of me. You have given me hope that I can become a decent man, that I can still have a life within society. I do not want to be an outcast anymore."

"I am the wrong person to come to if you think I am not an outcast!" Marian considered him for a moment. He had done the honest thing. It did not matter if it had come a little late. "You said this Arthur, he is a dangerous man to cross?" He nodded to confirm. "He would come after the both of us if you did not turn up?" He nodded once more but gave her a questioning look. A plan was forming in her mind.

"I thought you would throw me out. I lied to you. I am working for the outlaws who robbed your home." Marian could not understand why she trusted him, but she did. She had not thought herself capable of trust since her uncle.

"I owe you for last night. You saved me and now I am saving you. We will do as Arthur said. You will take me to him as bait for Gisbourne. He is a horrid man and I do not care what the outlaws do to him. But we will have our own plan as well. You will send word to your leader that Arthur is rebelling against him and contradicting his rules. Your leader will come and do as he sees fit to those who have wronged him." She felt powerful, a power she had never felt before. She was a leader, a strategist. She had finally had an opportunity to prove herself, to go on an adventure and test her skills. But she also felt naïve. Marian had never been in danger like this before, not willingly anyway. She had no idea whether her plan would work or not, but she had to try; there was little choice in it. In a way Marian felt selfish; she could have just left it and let her fate come to her, but she was doing this because she could – because she wanted to be a hero – and she hated herself for it.

"That is a damn good plan you have, if I do say so myself. I guess there is no way of stopping you? I do not want to put you in this position."

"How do you get messages to your leader?"

"There is an outlaw not too far from here, always scouting near Nottingham. Someone will need to pass on the message and show him this:" He pulled a chain from his pocket with a small symbol of a sideways 8 on. "He will know the threat is real and will pass the message on." Marian guessed they could not read or write, as most people could not. Very few even realised Marian was literate.

Marian called for Beatrice and Alice from the servants' quarters. She asked Alan to explain to Beatrice the directions of where to meet the messenger. Beatrice left immediately with the necklace. Then Marian took Alice to the side.

"Alice, I need you to do something for me. I do not have enough staff to help so I am sorry, but you will have to go out on your own."

Alice was very quiet. A few months ago, Alice's parents had been stabbed and left for dead. Nobody but Alice had witnessed their murder and the killer was still out there somewhere. Ever since, Marian and Beatrice had kept her away from the world, letting her deal with the past in peace and solitude. Alice did a few small tasks around Marian's home but only kitchen and cleaning duties to keep her occupied. Marian felt awful for pulling her into this situation, but she had no choice.

"What do I have to do?"

"I need you to deliver a message to Beatrice's friend, Emma, who works in the castle. She is a nice woman and does not live too far from here, next door to the baker. Tell Emma to find a way to let Gisbourne know that his love is in danger in the forest. She will know what to do. Okay?" Alice looked so small and vulnerable. Marian did not want to ask this of her.

"Yes. I can do that. I promise I will not let you down."

Marian prepared her horse for travel. Chestnut had been a gift from Walter to help her feel more secure when traveling around Nottingham, though she rarely rode, preferring to blend in and walk. Alan helped her up onto the front of Chestnut and then mounted behind her. She felt his heart beat against her back and her checks flushed. She was glad to be at the front where he could not see; she had never been so close to a man before.

Chapter 8

As they rode, Marian remained uncomfortably aware of the closeness of their bodies.

She knew one day she would have to marry; the only way she survived now was through Walter. If he ever died, she would want to marry someone she loved. She would not be able to bear marrying someone like Gisbourne.

She had not noticed before, but Alan was quite handsome. She looked at him as he rode, his eyes a deep brown. She looked away, having caught his eye, flushing even brighter than before. His whole face seemed to light up when he smiled. She was glad to have him. He could not help his circumstances. He was a friend and if she did not love anyone enough to marry them, she could quite happily marry him and learn to love him. She cared for him in the same way she cared for Walter. They were her family, and blood did not matter.

But how would she survive if she married someone like him? She could only marry someone she trusted, but Alan had no fixed job and a dark and dangerous past. She was providing him with an income and she could not rely on him to provide for her. She could certainly not live in the forest.

Marian was terrified of the forest and the memories it might awaken. She breathed deeply, trying to take her mind off what lay ahead. She hated the unknown; it worried her so much that some nights she would lay awake for hours afraid of the devil that haunted her sleep.

She prayed silently that her plan would work. Marian was risking so much but she had no choice. It was either go to Arthur or be hunted down. She already lived in fear of being found by her uncle. She did not want to add to that list. She had to put her faith in Alan if anything were to go wrong today. She had promised herself never to rely on anyone again and she was going directly against that instinct. It started a sickening feeling in her gut; promises meant very little to some people.

Marian looked at Alan through the corner of her eye. He was concentrating but she noticed a twitch at the edge of his mouth, the only sign of his uneasiness. That served to release a further sickness inside her that could not be tamed.

Alan stopped the horse. They were now near the deepest part of the forest, having strayed from the through roads. She stared into the unknown and swallowed hard. This was it, there was no turning back now.

Alan let out a sigh behind her. "Are you sure?"

Marian took a deep breath and after a moment's hesitation – this was the last chance to turn around and go home – she nodded, and the horse continued into the forest.

Internally, Marian was panicking but she did not want to look weak. She tried to breathe slowly but it was not working; she was too alert. A noise beside her and she tensed. A few birds flew out of the trees and Marian knew she was being paranoid, but she could not seem to control herself. Each and every sound made her jump, and she would have fallen off Chestnut if it were not for Alan's strong arms keeping her in place. He could probably sense her fear, but she did not care. There was nothing she could do to calm herself. Her heart raced faster with every stride the horse took. Her palms were slick with sweat and shaking. Marian held them tightly together, trying desperately to make them stop, but to no avail.

Her memories did not return, thankfully, one positive at least. The forest here looked different, and she was grateful for small mercies.

After a while longer, Alan stopped at the edge of a clearing and dismounted. He helped Marian from the horse and tied Chestnut to a nearby tree. Marian had to look weak and useless, just how Arthur would want. She struggled to get rid of her mask of indifference. It had taken her years to perfect it, but the barrier was torn down in mere seconds. Alan nodded to her – they were ready.

At once, several men appeared from the shadows. Alan turned her roughly in Arthur's direction. She felt a push behind her and knew what she had to do. She fell feebly to the ground, scraping her knees on twigs, but she barely felt it. Her senses were heightened, and she could feel the blood buzzing around her body. She was alive with energy. *Was this what it felt like to be a soldier?*

She felt naked in front of these rogues. They looked like they meant business, all their faces twisted and distorted into the hungry growls of wolves. Her eyes locked on one she recognised from the night they attempted to steal from her.

Arthur. She looked to his arm, where her arrow had struck home, a bandage still wrapped around the spot. She felt a sense of pride and almost smiled but at the last second stopped herself. She had to appear weak, she reminded herself. Marian could not take on all these men together even if she actually had a weapon. There must have been at least 15 to 20 of them. Arthur looked at her then and she shied away, for she could see the danger Alan had warned her about.

#

Alice knocked on Emma's door. It had taken her a while to get her bearings as she had hardly ventured out of the manor since she arrived in Nottingham. Nobody answered and she was just about to give up when the door creaked open, and a face peered around it. It was a woman, about the same age as Beatrice, not young but also not yet old. She had black hair and very pale skin, making her bony face look sharp enough to prick your finger. She looked suspiciously at Alice.

"Sorry Miss, my name is Alice. I am a friend of Beatrice and have come to you for help."

"My name is Emma. I am not important enough to have any title, though it was kind of you. Any friend of Beatrice's is a friend of mine. She has helped me so much." Emma opened the door wide, welcoming Alice inside.

Emma's home was a small room with a pile of straw in one corner, presumably the bed, where a young boy slept. He looked about eight years old with the same black hair and pale, sharp face as Emma's.

"My son. He is not very well but we cannot afford a physician. Beatrice often brings us medicine. My husband died of a similar illness to what George has, but Beatrice's medicine helps him sleep. He seems so much more peaceful when he sleeps," she contemplated. Alice felt great sympathy towards this woman who had nothing but was still grateful, nonetheless. "What can I help you with?"

"Could you please pass on a message to Gisbourne? His love has been taken by outlaws in the forest. I think that was it. Is there any way you could do this? It is really important."

"Of course, I would, but I cannot help. Gisbourne has gone away on business. He has told no one where he has gone or how long he will be. He left late last night. I am so sorry, but whatever this is, it will have to wait."

Alice suddenly felt helpless. The one thing she had been entrusted with, she could not even carry out. She had failed already, but she felt even worse for

Emma, who wanted so much to help and to pay Beatrice back in whatever small way possible. Alice put on a brave face.

"Thank you anyway. I must be off. Perhaps I will see you again soon. I will make sure more medicine is sent and will pray for your son when I speak to God."

"Thank you. You do not know how much it means to me. Please, if there is ever anything I can do, just come to me."

Emma was so polite, it made Alice feel even worse. She had such delicate manners, it was obvious she had learnt to only speak kindly and quietly working in the castle.

Emma opened the door carefully, peering around to check no guards were about, and then opened it wider for Alice to leave. As soon as the door shut behind Alice, she set off in a run. She did not know what she could do to help, but she had to get back to Marian's and hope somebody was there.

When Alice arrived home, her worries were realised. Beatrice was still on her errand and Alice had no choice but to help Marian. She could not leave her to a fate that could be avoided. She caught her breath and started off towards the forest. Marian had told her that a trail was being left to lead Gisbourne to Marian and the outlaws, so she simply followed it herself. Perhaps she would be too late. She quickened her pace just in case.

Chapter 9

Time was passing, and there was still no sign of Gisbourne. Marian had been planted near the far end of the clearing with the men hidden from view. She did not know how much time had passed, but she was growing tired and the energy that coursed through her veins a while ago had evaporated, and in its place only a sense of emptiness.

She licked her chapped lips, her mind drifting to darker thoughts as time went on; exploring every single possibility and only making the situation worse. She knew though, that Gisbourne did have feelings for her, no matter how corrupt they may be. She felt ill at the idea of his love for her.

She could sense Alan nearby, though he was hidden away in the trees. She could not understand an outlaw's life. How could they just rob innocents without a thought? Marian would never be capable of such a thing. Perhaps she could rob someone who deserved it, but how would you decide if they were deserving or not? Outlaws must have some sense of what is right and wrong. But she could see Alan cared, perhaps they had all hidden it deep inside out of necessity. She would probably never find out. She felt a pang of sympathy for them and quickly blotted it out. Most of them probably deserved to be outlaws, committing heinous crimes. But there must be others like Alan, she hoped.

Marian heard a commotion nearby in the direction Gisbourne was supposed to arrive from. Perhaps this was the moment. She prepared herself, her heart racing once again and adrenaline coursing through her veins. One of Arthur's men stepped out from the shadows, dragging someone. Marian gasped.

Alice squirmed against the rogue's rough grip on her dress. Marian could see the fear plain in her eyes, a reflection of her own expression. She wanted to run and help her, but she had no way of getting to her with her legs and arms bound, and the moment she tried to move, she knew that the rogues would come after her. At that thought, the rest of the men reappeared, with Arthur storming towards Alice. He yelled for the men to search her and Marian struggled to watch, uselessly.

Alice had more bravery than Marian had given her credit for. She was the last person Marian had ever expected to come storming into a place like this. She was ashamed for keeping her hidden away from the world for so long. Marian had always thought Alice was weak and now she hated herself for it. How could she create such a demeaning opinion of Alice based upon nothing but her past?

#

Alan stepped out into the clearing to see what all the fuss was about. He stopped suddenly as soon as he saw Alice. She had never spoken a word to him before. What was she doing here? He turned to Marian and her eyes moved between him and Alice frantically. It was clear Alice was not meant to be here, and she was in danger. He took a deep breath and rushed over to Alice.

"Wait!" Alan demanded, in such a powerful tone he prepared himself to be struck down by Arthur for speaking out of turn. He racked his brains for an excuse, but the truth would work fine. "This is the girl I sent to deliver the message to Gisbourne." He looked to Alice, concerned. "Why are you here? What happened?"

Arthur waved a hand at the rogue restraining Alice, who let her go instantly. She stumbled clumsily and Alan stepped forward ready to catch her. She caught her balance and looked into Arthur's eyes. Alan wondered if she had ever met anyone as terrifying as Arthur.

She went awfully pale, and Alan prepared himself to step in, but she met Arthur's glare. She did not seem afraid. This was different.

"He is away on business, Gisbourne I mean. I could not deliver the message... so... I... came here to let you know."

#

This man killed my parents. That was all Alice could think about. She thought she would be scared of him. She had feared that face for so long, ever since she had watched him burn down her family's home with them inside while he held her, forcing her to watch, hearing her parents cry for help. Now her blood boiled, and she wanted revenge. Pure hatred washed over her and all she could see was his laughing face, thinking he had won. He deserved to suffer. She took out the knife she kept in her pocket for safety. She heard Marian scream in the distance, but she could not back out of it now. She lunged at him, but someone pulled her back. She screamed and kicked out and then she was flying backwards at full force, hitting her head against something hard, then… darkness.

#

Marian could do nothing but shout as one of Arthur's men flung Alice like a ragdoll and she hit a tree with a thump, falling to the ground limp. Marian squirmed against her bindings, feeling them dig into her already sore wrists, only making her more aware of what was unfolding. She did not understand Alice's rage but she admired it. The rogues were walking towards Alice, ready to do real harm to her. She had only made them more vengeful. Marian looked to Alan with wild eyes, but he was too shocked to do anything, and then she opened her mouth.

"Wait, please! I am the one you want. She is nothing but a stupid child. I am the one who made you look weak and powerless against a girl." Marian could see that was not enough to sway him. She had to rile him up. "I told Gisbourne where you were. He knows everything. Better watch your back!" Marian lost all sense of self-preservation, a dangerous thing, but she needed this distraction. She had to save Alice.

Arthur's attention was on Marian now. Alan's warning went through her mind; Arthur could not control his anger. Marian was terrified but she could not take it back. The rogues started chanting and encouraging him; a part of her revelled in this. *Let him do his worst.*

Arthur pulled her up by the hair and whispered in her ear.

"I would let my men have you, but this is personal." His voice was cold and cruel, and sent a shiver through her body.

There was nothing she could do but brace herself. She closed her eyes, ready for impact. She prayed he would not go for her back. Even thinking about it made her scars throb with the memory of the pain. She heard a loud thump and fell to the floor. She had not felt anything. She opened her eyes, disoriented.

Alan was standing, looking down at Arthur, who lay a few feet away from her. Arthur glared back at Alan, daring him. All was silent around them as the others stared in disbelief. No one risked standing up against Arthur and they did not know what to do when someone did. Arthur's gaze turned to Marian. Their cover was blown, he knew they were working together.

"Restrain them!" he yelled across the clearing. In an instant, the scene turned from silent horror to pure chaos.

Marian felt rough hands on her arms, pulling her to her feet. A few men held Alan in place and her heart fell to her stomach. Arthur approached Alan, and Marian desperately tried to wriggle free, but the rough man's hands tightened to the point of pain.

"You fool! You let the witch play with your mind. We do not need a weakling like you. I will finish you." Arthur grabbed a dagger off one of his men. "I am going to make this slow and very painful." Arthur dragged the 'very' out, and her stomach twisted in knots. Then she heard shouts from his men.

"What about her?"

"She ruined your plans. She deserves it too!"

Marian watched Arthur carefully as he considered it, then threw the thought aside. His mind was made up. He would not look weak in front of his men.

"You have her then! She is all yours! My treat." He smiled; a dark, ugly smile and Marian knew what it meant.

She tried to block out her fear and forget what was about to happen, but she could not shake her terror. She pushed against the man's strong grip, trying to get away, but it was pointless. Alice was in her vision; she had just regained consciousness. Alice caught her helpless gaze, but Marian only shook her head. She did not want Alice involved in this. Alice understood though and lay still on the ground.

All of the men, apart from the two holding Alan in place, started towards her hungrily. She heard a clang of metal behind her and knew, without looking, that the one holding her had a weapon, probably a dagger. He let go of her with one hand, but she had nowhere to go. She was surrounded and she could not escape if she tried. Before she realised what he was doing, she felt something warm dripping down her arm. She looked down, suddenly hazy, and noticed a slash down her left sleeve and a shallow cut from the impact of the dagger. She felt a push and stumbled forward, losing balance. Marian felt empty and broken, nothing left to fight. She fell to the floor with a thump, not even thinking to put her hands up to soften the fall. She felt the impact rush through her as though she had just fallen from a great height.

Another of the rogues pulled her back up. Somewhere in her mind, blocked off from pure fright, she noticed he held no weapon. But she could not seem to connect her body to her thoughts. She was living a new kind of nightmare. The rogue turned her to face him. She could not bear to see the expression on his face, so she looked to the ground instead, hoping she would wake up. Then she was pushed backwards and landed in another's arms.

She felt a tug at the back of her dress and heard a rip.

A breeze found the scars on Marian's back and she shivered. Her face paled and the world spun around her. But still she stood, unable to control herself. She heard a gasp from behind her and she was suddenly free. She should have run, but any energy she had left drained out of her. She dropped back onto her knees. She faintly heard someone ask if she had performed some sort of witchcraft on him. Her ears thrummed in the madness. She looked over to Alan and was relieved to see him fighting. She tried to focus on him, to regain some level of conscious thought. Alan looked like a decent fighter. She attempted to strategize, as she had taught herself. He had managed to get hold of a dagger, taken from the rogue lying on the floor. At least Alan was alright.

Marian returned to her immediate threats. Her ears burned but they were no longer thrumming. She took a deep breath and tried to focus. The men chanted names at her:

'impure', 'dirty', and 'deformed' were amongst them. She was overly aware of her back. It was bare and she felt naked and ashamed. Even these brutes would not take her. Once more, the scars from her past stopped her from having a future. Her whole body throbbed so painfully she cried out before she could stop the sound.

#

Alan fought hard against Arthur. He had to get to Marian and protect her. He had put her in danger's path and promised to keep her safe. He was failing but he had to get to her.

The rogues holding him had been surprised when he thrashed out with his legs, sending them flying. He had managed to yank a knife out of one of their hands in the process and they had underestimated him. They should have known that, with his background, he would have some weaponry skills. But he had not seen most of these rogues before. With a sense of dread, he realised Arthur's army must be growing by the day. How could such a man inspire so much loyalty? The answer was plain to see, though. They all feared Arthur, and he knew it. But Alan had watched Arthur training and fighting. He had seen how Arthur always chose the sword over a dagger. He hoped this would play to his advantage. Then a huge voice rang across the clearing and the world went silent.

Alan would recognise that voice from anywhere. Marian's plan had worked. Their true leader had arrived.

Chapter 10

"What do you think you are doing?!" His voice boomed across the clearing, stopping everyone in their tracks. To Marian, it looked like time had stopped in an instant. Relief washed over her as she looked around, shock emanating from the rogues faces. Even Arthur was still, Marian noticed with a smile creeping over her lips. She searched for the man who had just spoken, but she could not see past the rogues. Her eyes focused on Alan, his expression similar to Marian's. *This must be the leader he was talking about.* From the shadows, she saw at least 30 men appear, surrounding the rogues.

"Arthur step forward." Arthur shuffled towards the voice that Marian could not put a face to. "You have directly betrayed my authority, making my men your personal slaves, to do your dirty work for you. I took you in out of respect and kindness and you have deceived me. Do not think you can make an excuse for your actions. There is no reasoning for such treachery." The man paused for a moment, and Marian watched Arthur closely. His face twitched, irritated. "Because I once knew you as a better man, I will allow you to leave and go about your ways... elsewhere. If, however, myself or my men cross paths with you again, you will be killed without question. That goes for the rest of you too. I could never trust such men who would be so easily misled. Alan, however, you have done a great service to me and you are welcome to stay."

Marian felt no pity for these rogues; they deserved to be hung for all she cared. Now *this* man was a true leader. He did not command loyalty through fear, but with mutual respect. This was the most powerful type of loyalty and Marian could see it plain in the rogues' faces. They knew they had made a great mistake. Slowly they dispersed, some rushing in case he was not true to his word.

Jolting from a touch to her shoulder, Marian turned quickly, only to see Alan. Without a word, he removed his jacket and carefully placed it over her shoulders, covering her back.

She felt utterly vulnerable, but she was safe now. Then Alice was next to her.

"Are you alright?" Alice asked.

Marian could see she had blossomed into a woman, independent and brave. She was strong in a way Marian had not been at that age, and even now. Marian realised with relief that Alice had not seen her scars, thanks to Alan's quick thinking. It was one less thing to explain, at least. She could not believe that this young woman before her was Alice, the traumatised little girl. Marian could not hide the effects of the day though, as her hands shook fiercely and a great exhaustion came upon her.

"I should ask you the same," Marian replied shakily.

Neither knew what to say, so instead they sat in silence. Marian was grateful for small mercies. She would not have to explain anything now at least.

The clearing was nearly empty and the leader must have sent many of his men away, as only a few patrolled the edges. Marian was feeling weaker by the minute but did not want to complain. She tried to keep herself sat upright but Alan must have noticed her fading and sat beside her, letting her lean on him. Alice was sat a little away from them, staring off into the darkness of the forest, deep in thought. Marian's arm throbbed and she focused on the pain in an attempt to stay conscious.

Marian was unaware of time passing, but she felt herself slipping out of consciousness. At some point, Alan whispered that it would not be long. She could not gather the energy to ask what he was referring to. All she wanted was to be in the safety of her own home, in her own bed.

"Who is she, Alan?" Marian woke with a start and the leader loomed over her. She looked up, blinking away sleep. She recognised him instantly.

Robin Hood: the hero who was going to save her from the clutches of her uncle all those years ago. Marian had almost made it to him, but her uncle had caught her, and when she finally got away, he was long gone. Ever since, she had hoped to see him again. She had often wondered how her life might have panned out differently if she had escaped with him that day. He had come up with her outlaw name, Marian, which had inspired her new life with Walter. Even though she had only ever known Robin for a day, that day was the most vivid memory she could recall. She could remember the rush of excitement at the prospect of escaping her uncle and a new life where they would grow up together. She might not be here today, if she had never have met him.

She realised she had been staring too long, but before she could turn away, he was staring back at her.

His eyes widened for a moment and Marian's heart leaped with joy. He recognised her and she felt as light as a feather, all the weight lifted from her shoulders. He was a rugged sort of handsome, thin but muscular, and his eyes were the same bright green tint that stood out compared to his dull worn clothes. Now he wore well-fitted clothes, though they looked to be the same dull colour. She blushed as she realised he was no longer the little boy she had met in the forest, but a man. She must look so silly and small to him. Marian had not been in any immediate danger for years and this man lived in danger every day of his life.

"Mary? What are you doing here?" His voice was rough and deep, very unlike the squeaky, cheerful voice of his youth. He did not sound pleased to see her, as she had hoped, but instead wary and impatient. Her heart dropped instantly. She just wanted to be home; she did not have the energy for this. Perhaps he had not thought of her since that day, and at that thought she felt as lifeless as she had a few moments before. The nervous excitement had gone, leaving her hollow.

"I go by Marian these days," she said, looking at him through blurry eyes, trying to figure him out. She did not know what else to say. He seemed distant and disconnected.

"Mary?" Alice wondered. Only then did Marian realise Alice was still here, watching everything. Marian had not told anyone her old name, not even Walter knew it. She was still scared that someone from her old life would find her and take her back.

Robin had not moved and was looking behind her. He opened his mouth as though to speak, but no words came out. She looked away; he did not want her.

"I need to speak with you," she heard Alan say, somewhere in the distance. She let Alan wonder off with Robin. Marian sighed inwardly. It had been a day of adrenaline, fear and disappointment. It was too much to take in.

#

Alan told Robin everything that had happened and especially how Marian had become involved in it all. Robin gave nothing away as to how he knew Marian, and why he had called her Mary. It seemed too much of a coincidence and it made him uneasy. Alan suspected that they must have once had feelings for each other as Marian's face had lit up when she recognised him. They must

59

not have seen one another for many years though, by the shock emanating from their expressions. Perhaps this was Robin's past, although he knew Robin had been an outlaw since he was a child. Once Alan had explained what had led up to today, Robin looked weary, as though a great burden had been put upon him.

"What is it you want, Alan?" he asked with a sigh.

"You know I never wanted this life for myself. You saw, when I arrived, how much I wanted a normal life again. I was not cut out for life in the forest. Thanks to Marian's generosity, I can start to make a decent life for myself. I work for Marian and I am quite happy there. I owe her after today as well. This was all her plan." For some reason, he felt the need to back Marian up. The look Robin had given her earlier was more impatience than admiration.

She deserved better than that.

"It is your life. I will not stop you. I wish you every success. Now please escort the ladies home. This is no place for them." He was unengaged with his speech, his mind elsewhere. He walked off.

Alan wished he had asked Robin about Marian's past. Perhaps he knew what had caused her scars. But there was no point in asking; he knew when to keep his mouth shut.

#

Marian watched as Robin walked away in the distance. He did not even glance back at her, leaving her with a certainty that he did not care. Her arm throbbed, pulsing in time with her heartbeat. She looked to Alice, who was drained of colour.

"How is your head?" She still felt like a mother to her, and it was hard to shake off the desire to keep her safe.

"Sore, but I will be fine. I think we should get you home though, and get your wounds tended to." She sounded concerned, though Marian could not process it. She felt ready to drift off into nothingness.

The sun was going down as Alan returned with Chestnut. He helped Alice up first and then carefully picked Marian up and placed her behind Alice. Marian could not stay awake any longer. She leant forward and rested on Alice's back. All she could feel was the steady pace of the horse and Alan's footsteps next to them, leading them home to safety.

Chapter 11

Robin could not get his head around Arthur a Bland's deception. He had known Arthur for about five years now, and he had been one of his most trusted men. Robin should have expected it in a way, all the signs had always been there. The first time they met, Arthur had outsmarted him.

On the day he met Arthur, Robin had walked the same route he always did, ever since the outlaws moved deeper into the forest. He knew they were based somewhere between Birmingham and Coventry, though they never went close to the towns, but Robin would sometimes wonder around the borders and watch families, happy and loving. He used to think the outlaws were his family. Their leader, Connor, was Robin's father and he thought he knew what that had meant, until he had seen other families. Connor had never been caring or affectionate towards Robin, but he demanded loyalty from his men. His father did not become very close to any of the other outlaws, but he did pay some special attention to Robin. He had personally trained him and often scolded him for using the wrong techniques. It was helping him to grow as a leader. Connor had always made that clear to him, but he did not feel prepared for it. His father was no longer a fit, youthful man. His head was unclear and he slurred his words, but whenever anyone tried to get him a healer, he would refuse and insist he was fine.

Robin reminisced to a time long forgotten, when he was five years old, living in a huge manor, the location long forgotten. He missed the life of luxury, an easy lifestyle where they did not even need to provide for themselves. His father had been a Lord, raising Robert up alone, although he had rarely seen him, as he had a maid care for him instead. Robin's mother had died during childbirth, as many did, and not even wealth could hold off death. Then suddenly one day guards burst into the manor, shouting at his father to leave and never return. It turned out his father had been having an affair with the wife of the Sheriff, and they were gone, just like that. They tried to move towns, but everyone had heard of his father's dalliances; the Sheriff had made sure he paid for what he had done.

He had even gone so far as to burn the whole manor down, to destroy any trace they ever lived there. Robin could still not forgive his father, but he did respect him for building a community in the forest, making their own home, as meagre as it was.

On the fateful day Robin met Arthur, he had been walking to get some peace and quiet when he stopped abruptly; something did not feel right. He could feel eyes on him and he readied his sword. He was more comfortable with a bow, but dense woodland surrounded him and he could not shoot at close range. A man of a small, broad build appeared in front of him.

"Please, help me. You have to help me. He is after me!" The man fell to his knees, physically begging. Robin, who trusted no one, held his sword to the man's neck. The man did not flinch. "Or kill me. Please. He cannot reach me in death." This man in front of Robin was weak and worthless. Robin sheathed his sword and walked around the man, leaving him to be found by whoever was after him. The man might be on the run from authority and he did not want to get caught up in that.

Robin heard footsteps behind him and looked to find the man was following him.

"I will do anything, please keep me safe."

"No. I need no favours from a weasel like yourself."

"But I can prove myself. Let me explain," he begged.

"Well, answer me this: why are you being chased?" Robin quickened his pace, but turned away from the direction of camp, to ensure nobody would find their hideout. He loved adventure and had not really met anyone new for a while. He decided to play along to cure his boredom. The man huffed to keep up with him. It amused him to see such a weakling in the forest. He would not last long with or without his help.

"I stole from a very important person," an unexpected answer to Robin.

"*You* stole? I would not think you capable," he joked, for the first time in a while.

"Well, I did not steal it myself."

"Then why did you just lie to me? You seem to be in a bit of a pickle there. Best start digging your grave."

"A friend stole it and gave it to me, but the man he stole it from found out it was me and now he is after me!"

"So, this *friend* set you up. You really are a fool. Who did you, they, steal it from?"

"He is trusted by Prince John. A man named Gisbourne in his private guard."

"Continue. I love a good story, though you are not telling it very well…" Robin enjoyed teasing people. His father rarely allowed such comradery in camp.

"The prince gives gifts to his closest allies for their loyalty. My friend heard news of Gisbourne having been given a precious stone by Prince John himself. I have it here." He searched his pocket with shaking hands and showed Robin a bright red stone that glimmered.

Robin could not take his eyes off it. It must be worth a fortune. A grand idea was forming.

"Let me look after it for you, and when this Gisbourne finds you, he will search you and find you do not have it. I, at least, know how to defend myself should he come anywhere near me."

"Are you sure it will work?" He sounded uncertain.

"Absolutely," Robin tried to sound genuine, when internally he was laughing at the idiot. The man gave Robin the gem. "Now you run that way and I go the opposite, then you are separate from the gem and cannot be caught." He laughed to himself as he ran back to camp with riches to show off. Perhaps he might impress his father after all.

Robin arrived back at the camp in no time at all. All the men were still away on a mission to steal from a cart of goods that was travelling nearby. He started to make his way out the other end of camp and through a small, separate clearing where his father usually stayed, away from the rest of the gang.

As he entered the smaller clearing, he saw his father asleep near the fire. It was the middle of the day and this just made Robin worry more that soon his father would be gone and he would become the leader. He did not want to disturb him so sat beside him for a few minutes.

Just as Robin was about to give in to his pride and wake Connor, someone entered the clearing. He turned, expecting it to be his fellow outlaws returning but it was too quiet. He had been too big headed about the situation. Somehow, the man had followed him. He should have guessed that it was all an act, but he only felt angry at himself for being so confident; he was amazed by the deceptiveness of the man before him; this small, clever man would be an asset to the gang.

"You outwitted me," Robin exclaimed. "Here, you have earned your gem back. But consider joining our gang." The man took the gem hesitantly, waiting for retaliation, but Robin simply let him take it and raised his hands to show he would not attempt to fight him.

"I have enough problems to deal with. I do not want the burden of yours as well."

And at that, the man fled.

Robin turned to see his father awake, watching his son intently.

"Well done," Connor said sarcastically. "You have managed to fail and disappoint me in the space of seconds. I should have known all along. You are too weak to lead."

Robin felt his father's disappointment through to his bones. Before he could reply, he heard footsteps running towards them from the same direction the man had appeared. A tall, muscular man clad in black armour entered the camp. He looked very important and Robin's heart began to race. He was certain this was the person the man had been running from; Gisbourne. Robin had heard the name in passing tales of Prince John; he was a ruthless outlaw hunter. Robin gripped his sword in his hands, blunt and worn but still able to harm or even kill a person. Gisbourne stopped in front of him and glared, his eyes burning into Robin's soul. This was not a person he wanted to mess with.

"Look, I want no trouble. The man who has your gem went that way." Robin pointed the opposite direction to where the man had run. He did not know why, but he had a lot of respect for a man who could deceive even him.

Gisbourne seemed to stare a little too long at Robin, trying to decide whether to kill him or not. It must have been obvious to Gisbourne that he was an outlaw. Robin heard a thump behind him and he turned instinctively. Connor must have tried to stand and had collapsed on the ground. Robin ran over to him forgetting about Gisbourne. He turned, as he remembered that you should never turn your back on your enemy, but he had vanished.

Relieved, Robin turned his attention back to his father, but it was too late. His body and mind had finally given up on him. Robin did not feel the sadness of loss, only the terror that he might one day become as cold and calculating as his father.

When the men returned, Robin would be named the next leader. That had been the biggest, most terrifying day of his life and he would never forget that now there were worse memories entwined with that unfortunate day.

Around a year after he became the new leader, Robin had been preparing his gang to steal from a merchant's cart travelling through their neck of the woods. One of his lookouts had said it was unguarded and an older man steered the horse by himself. It would not be worth much, but they were running low on supplies and anything would do at this stage. He was finding it almost impossible to lead men that were hungry for food and adventure and had not a lot of either. In recent months, it had been quiet in the forest, so quiet that Robin was considering moving camp to a better location. But everyone seemed afraid of the forest and stuck to longer, safer routes, knowing of the outlaws that lurked on the forest paths.

There was a commotion near the site where they expected the cart to be, and the men slowed, following Robin as he crawled to the ground and peered over to the road below them. Someone had beaten them to the cart. A small, rounded man was threatening the driver with a knife. Robin put out a hand to his men, to remain unseen for a moment. The elderly man was begging him not to take his cart. The man slit his throat and started searching the cart for goods. Robin whispered orders to get the cart for themselves and they ran down the slope silently. As they reached the cart, the man was getting comfortable holding the reins and ready to ride off. Robin grabbed him and pulled him out.

The man looked at Robin with a look of greed.

"You are surrounded," Robin pointed out, his men surrounding them both.

The man's look changed and he beamed a brilliant smile. "Brother, it is me. You helped me get away from Gisbourne with that gem I stole."

"Well, I can see it fed you well, although you told me you did not steal it!"

"But I did! I fooled you again!"

Robin laughed, easing. It was the man he saved from Gisbourne, who had managed to deceive the great Robin Hood. "Men, stand down," Robin ordered. "He is a friend. This man once bested me." He turned back to the man. "Please, join us."

"Will you protect me if I join you?"

"Who is after you this time?" Robin joked.

"Gisbourne, he is still after me. I will help you any way I can." He seemed serious, not like his usual deceptiveness, but it was hard to tell. Robin decided to take his word for it.

This man would not have agreed to join the gang if it were not for good reason.

"Of course, I have not forgotten your abilities. Welcome to my gang. I do not even know your name."

"I am sorry. My name is Arthur a Bland."

Robin shivered at the memory. If only he had not invited Arthur into the gang, then none of this would have happened. He had trusted him with his men, to bring in extra money and supplies from a separate camp near Nottingham. But he had had no idea Arthur had been recruiting Robin's own men to turn against him. He should have known not to trust Arthur, after all, their first encounter had been a deception. Since their first meeting, Robin had heard of many incidents between his men and Gisbourne, some of his own men had even been killed by Gisbourne, and for no reason, it seemed now. He had been protecting a predator who deserved to be hunted down by Gisbourne.

Robin could feel his authority diminishing and his world was falling apart. All he had was his gang and without them he would not know what to do with his life. He had no idea how to inspire his men after this betrayal though. Robin had been the man to let Arthur into his gang, and everyone had suffered because of it. Arthur had stolen some of his best men, and the only person who had saved him was Alan. He owed Alan and wanted him close; he was the only person he trusted. But he had to let Alan do what he wanted; it was the right thing to do. Now he only had a small group of trusted men, the smallest group he had ever had. Will Scarlett and Little John were the only ones truly loyal to him. Everyone else did as they pleased, and he worried that one day they would all desert him.

Then there was Marian. She had thrown everything off. How was she involved in all of this? He had put that part of his life behind him, and now it was haunting him. He tried to block out all the emotions stirred by the sight of her after so many years. His father would hate how weak he had become, and he had been right all along; Robin was no leader.

Chapter 12

Marian awoke to hushed voices outside her room. She could not remember the journey home, only the sensation of falling into an abyss as she slept feverishly. It was dark outside, but candles were lit around her chamber. She tried to turn onto her back, but pain seared from her old scars and she gasped, rolling back onto her side. The door opened and Beatrice rushed in. Marian felt like crying, but she would not allow herself to fall apart in such a way that would leave her vulnerable. Robert, her physician, followed Beatrice into the room. He sat on the chair next to Marian and watched her.

"Marian, I wish you would give me some explanation. A part of your history? How you got the scars?" He was attempting to break the barrier she had spent so long putting up between herself and others. He was trying her patience as always, and she did not feel up to fighting him. She understood that him knowing what had happened in her past might help him understand her pain, but it caused her too much internal pain to even think about, let alone speak it. She looked away from his judging face, towards the door, where she noticed Alan, with his back turned away from her. Robert was talking to her, probing her to tell him something, but she was not listening. She could hear the laboured sound of her own breathing. It was bringing too many emotions, too many memories back to life.

She snapped out of it the moment Alan spoke.

"She does not owe anyone an explanation. We all have secrets, things that are best left unsaid. I think you have helped Marian all you can. If we need you again, we will send for you. Beatrice, show him the way out."

Marian could sense Beatrice's frustration as she took her time in leaving the room; she did not like to be bossed around. Marian was relieved that at least Beatrice was her usual feisty self. Beatrice shut the door behind her carefully, leaving Marian in peace.

Marian sighed in relief. She liked Alan's company. He was happy to wait in silence until Marian wanted to talk.

"I am sorry you had to see that," she said finally.

"See what?"

"The… the scars. I would not have wished anyone to see them."

"You owe me nothing. You do not have to talk about this."

"But I need to speak to someone. I cut myself off from the world and do not trust anyone. I need to be able to trust someone. Too long I spend listening to gossip, the rumours; I start to believe them after a while. I forget who I really am and become someone else. I hide the truth even from myself. I need someone I can talk to about… anything. I choose you."

"Marian. Rest now. We can speak tomorrow. I will always listen." Alan was too kind, too honest for her. They had already been through so much together, and he had stuck with her through his own choice, leaving behind his old life to be with her.

"Thank you. Do you mind staying? I sometimes get…"

"Of course." He sat beside her before she could finish.

I am running, so fast the wind hits my face and I struggle to breathe. I must be running from uncle, but I look back to check. I halt, staring. Time stands still. Robin is there.

He freezes when he sees me. I hope, I pray he will come to me, talk to me, anything. He stares blankly; he does not recognise me. I could be his enemy. Then he turns and walks away.

Marian. I am alone. Marian. The world shakes.

Marian opened her eyes and Alan was right there, holding her hand tightly. Sweat clung to her and her hair stuck to her face.

"Do you get those a lot?"

"Did you sleep at all?" she whispered, her mouth dry. She tried to catch her breath.

"I slept enough. Do you have nightmares often?"

"Not that one, usually the past. I expect the past. That was… different." She stayed silent for a moment, trying to work out what it meant. She had a habit of working out what her nightmares meant. She was scared… terrified even… of being alone.

"Are you hungry? I could ask Beatrice to cook something up for you?"

"Can you ask Beatrice to come up? I have things to do. I need to get ready."

"Robert said you need to rest and take it easy. You do not want another of his lectures, do you?"

"I *will* take it easy. Please get Beatrice and have some time to yourself," she snapped, more harshly than she had meant.

He left and almost instantly, Beatrice arrived. She tried to distract Marian with the usual drivel of town gossip, of who is betrothed to whom, lots of names she did not recognise and lives she did not care about. Marian had not told Beatrice anything of the previous night, and she was relieved when she did not attempt to find out.

Marian could not stop thinking about Robin and the way he had looked at her: disgust, disinterest, hatred? She could not tell his emotions. She should try to let it go, but she could not get him out of her head. She had imagined meeting him so many times and never had that scenario come up. She had always expected him to have thought about her often, wondered about her life. But obviously, it was one sided. Beatrice dressed Marian in a loose-fitting dress, as usual very plain and unnoticeable.

"Would you mind showing me to Alice's room?" Marian asked kindly.

"You should not set foot in the servants' quarters. It is not right for a Lady," Beatrice replied, too formally.

"Beatrice, you know I am no Lady. Please, I need to speak to her, on her own terms." Marian smiled, knowing Beatrice would never say no to her.

Beatrice offered a hand to Marian to help her down the stairs, but she ignored it, pushing herself to be strong. She should have accepted the help; every step sent a shockwave of pain pulsing through her body. Beatrice kept watch in case Marian needed her. She led Marian to Alice's room.

In all these years, Marian had never set foot in the servants' quarters. Originally Marian had asked Beatrice to live upstairs in the extra bed chamber, but she had refused, announcing it was no place for a maid, that it was frowned upon. Beatrice never wanted Marian to see the type of accommodation maids lived in, and she had always stayed away, as it was their right to privacy. But Marian wanted Alice to feel comfortable talking to her, and the only place where Alice could possibly feel most at ease was in her own chambers.

Beatrice stopped at the door and gave it a tap. She left Marian at that moment, uttering an excuse about something or other.

After a few moments, Alice opened the door, just enough to peer around and see who was outside. As soon as she noticed Marian, she opened it wide. She looked surprised and out of sorts.

#

Alice did not understand why Marian was coming to her room, but she felt vulnerable letting Marian in, as though her room might reveal something private.

"Marian, what can I do for you?" She tried to act professional, just like Beatrice.

"I would like to speak to you privately. May I come in?" An odd request, but she would never say no to Marian.

"Well, of course. I apologise for the mess." Alice noted the way Marian walked. Usually she took strides, and Alice had always watched in amazement at her confidence. But this was different. Beatrice had whisked Alan carrying Marian upstairs as soon as they had arrived home last night, and she had heard no news since. Beatrice had never let Alice dress Marian before, perhaps she thought her incapable. But she had always thought they were hiding something from her. Now Marian walked carefully, as though it hurt to put one foot in front of the other, but Marian would never show such weakness.

Alice had never had a guest before; she did not know how to act. Marian stood inside the room. The whole situation seemed wrong; Marian was always the one to accept guests.

"Please take a seat." It felt strange for a servant to offer her Lady a seat. Alice moved the stool from the corner of the room close to the bed. She sat on the bed and watched as Marian sat, very slowly, and noticed a small twitch in her eyes, a silent wince of pain.

"I would like to talk to you about last night. I have a few questions. You do not have to answer them. It is selfish but I am curious. What made you attack that rogue Arthur yesterday? Your courage came out of nowhere."

"He killed my parents," Alice blurted out before she could stop herself. In a way, it was a relief to get it off her chest and say it out loud. Suddenly last night seemed all too real. She could feel her anger rising again, and she desperately tried to keep it at bay. She looked at the floor trying to focus. It was too quiet. After a few moments, she looked up to see what Marian's reaction would be.

"I see. You know, I used to hold a lot of anger against those who hurt me, just like you. I hated feeling weak and useless. That is why I took to learning to defend myself. It might help you too. I would love to teach you some skills. In all honesty, it would help me to have the company."

Out of all the things Marian might come to her about, Alice had not expected this. She thought Marian would be angry at her for putting them all in danger.

"I would love that!" She realised after she said it that she sounded like an excited little child, but she did not care. A distraction was just what she needed.

"I have a few errands to run today. Have you seen Alan?" And just like that, Marian was onto another task. She was always such a busy woman. Alice wished she could one day be as important as her.

"I heard him outside a few minutes ago."

"Please take it easy today. We have all been through a lot."

"You too, Marian." For the first time, it felt natural for Alice to call Marian by her first name. It was something she had always felt awkward about, not really knowing her very well, but now they shared something. Everything was changing, for the better, she hoped.

#

Marian left Alice to her thoughts and found Alan where she said he would be. He was by Marian's training area, throwing knives at a tree. She knew he would be able to sense she was there but he did not say anything, just carried on throwing knives until he had none left. Marian leant against the wall, trying to ease the aches in her body. He walked towards the tree and pulled the knives out, before turning and walking to stand next to Marian.

"I was just thinking, yesterday Robin recognised you. It is a small world," he wondered thoughtfully.

"Feeling pushy today Alan? 'I was just thinking…'" she mocked, jokingly. He meant well, and he would be curious, just like she had been with Alice. "I knew him in another life. I do not even think we really knew each other. You cannot know someone after only a few hours. I was going to run off with the outlaws when I was young. The day I met him changed my life. If it were not for him, I would probably never have escaped. He gave me courage when I had nothing left."

"It sounds like you did know each other very well."

"He has changed a lot. I always wondered about him. Now at least I know he is a successful... outlaw?"

"A successful outlaw, eh?" He laughed, a full bellied laugh that made Marian smile.

"He seems so serious now. He used to be an adventurer, battling imaginary beasts.

"But times change, people change. I changed. He changed. It was another life back then."

"If it is any consolation, he was an adventurer when I first joined his father's gang. His father's death changed a lot of things. He seems to have lost his heart, his soul. Being a leader is a great burden on him. He is trying so desperately to be like his father or not be like him, when he should just be himself."

"That is a thoughtful way of looking at things. Everyone becomes lost at some point in their lives. Finding your way back is the hard part."

Marian and Alan stayed side by side, thinking about their lives up to this point, the choices they had made. In blissful silence, they enjoyed each other's company, wondering what the future had in store for them.

Chapter 13

Everything went back to normal fairly quickly for Marian. She started training Alice as soon as she was back to herself. It turned out Alice was quite good company. Marian still could not bring herself to speak much of her past but became more trusting of Alice and Alan and everything was going well. Marian could not shake a bad feeling in her gut though. She had not seen Gisbourne since the night he showed up unannounced, and she was happy about it, but it seemed odd to her. He had accepted the challenge to romance her and done nothing about it. He was planning something, and she had no way of finding out until he returned.

She had not gone to see Walter in the castle either. She was worried about him but could not bring herself to see him. Something kept her away but she could not put her finger on it. Marian felt uneasy, her body sizzling with unwanted energy. The more time that passed, the more the feeling grew. She was on edge, ready to defend or attack as if there were a threat around every corner. She had spent her whole life sleeping with one eye open, preparing herself for anything. The rogue outlaws were gone and Gisbourne was leaving her alone. She should be happy, but she could not shake the feeling that something bad was going to happen. She spent all her time training, preparing for every eventuality.

Then it happened. Something even Marian could not train herself for.

As Beatrice was dressing Marian one morning, Alice raced up the stairs.

"He just stormed in. I could not stop him. He says he has urgent news."

"Who?"

"Gisbourne!"

Marian let Beatrice quickly finish dressing her and rushed downstairs. Marian would have loved to keep him waiting, but it sounded important. Gisbourne paced the room, unsettled, and it only fed her anxieties more.

"What is it?" Marian demanded, if only to help her release the tension building inside.

Gisbourne stopped in his tracks and looked at her. It was the first time she had ever seen something other than anger in his eyes. He seemed sombre, but Marian could not decide if it was genuine or not.

"I suggest you sit down for this news." His voice sounded soft and surprising to Marian. She only expected him capable of anger and power, but not comfort. Perhaps she had misjudged him after all.

"I am fine standing. For goodness' sake, speak!" She flinched the moment the words came out of her mouth, remembering his quick temper. Marian glanced to Alan, who was lingering in the corner of the room. He looked just as uncertain as she felt.

"Alright…" Gisbourne spoke unsurely. "I am afraid that I bring bad news. The Sheriff has died. I know you were close. I am here for you if you need anything." He strung out the word 'anything' and Marian held on to that, trying to focus on something other than the nightmare that had just unravelled in front of her. Emptiness clung to her, as though she might disappear completely. She heard a buzzing in her ears and the focus slipped away. But still no tears came. Anger and shame replaced the emptiness inside. Marian knew she should have seen Walter sooner. She could tell he had been weak and weary, but she had not wanted to face it. And now it was too late. She closed her eyes for a second to try to clear her head.

Strategize. I must think like a warrior. I have trained myself for this. Block the emotions out.

Clear the mind. Take a deep breath.

"Alice, go to Robert and escort him straight to the castle." She turned to Gisbourne, forgetting her disdain for him momentarily. "Gisbourne, do you have your carriage with you?"

"Of course, but you should be grieving. You need not burden yourself with this. It is a man's job." The look Marian gave quieted him. His thoughts were so blatantly obvious to her now. That was his way of proving himself to her. She needed Gisbourne to trust her, though. She knew something had been going on in the castle, but she could not afford to make him suspicious.

"I will grieve in my own time. Right now, I wish to go to the castle and make the necessary arrangements myself. Please escort me to the castle. Alan, I will be in need of your assistance as well."

I must stay strong. It is what Walter would have wanted.

Before Marian had time to think what lay ahead at the castle for her, they were already there. In silence, she jumped off the carriage, ignoring Gisbourne's hand to help her down. With a huff, he fell in behind her, and Marian could sense Alan behind him, watching and waiting for any sign of hostility. The castle was eerily quiet. There was no one in charge anymore and nothing for the staff to do but wait. Marian marched straight to Walter's chambers, where he had died. Just as Marian was about to open the door, she realised Alan and Gisbourne were still there. This was something she had to do alone. Without even acknowledging them, she said:

"Wait here."

For the first time, Gisbourne actually obeyed. She had half expected him to waltz in after her, arguing that a lady should not see a corpse, but he did not, and it meant he might have an ounce of humanity after all. It made Marian wonder if Gisbourne had seen loss before. To be such an unforgiving man, something bad must start you off on the path of destruction.

As Marian entered the room, she noticed a difference. It no longer made her feel warm and loved, but instead the room was dark and damp. Walter was lying on the bed, where she could have mistaken him for sleeping if he had not been so frighteningly still. She could feel a rising anger building inside her again, but she forced herself to continue, trying not to think of Walter as a person she loved. A potent smell lingered in the room, she thought it might be the smell of death, but she did not remember her mother's room smelling like this when she had died. The sensations were too much for her. This was not just another nightmare. It was real. To prove it to herself, she touched Walter's arm, ever so gently, afraid to wake him up, even though she knew he would never wake again. Her hand moved down to his hand and she suddenly pulled away. A memory sprang to life, of her mother's death, holding her hand, saying goodbye. She did not even get to say goodbye to Walter. *Focus.*

She could not help herself. She stroked his cheek, wishing him alive.

"I am sorry I was not there when you needed me," she whispered.

"...you are not authorised to inspect him. We have our own people to do that."

Gisbourne's voice cut into her grief.

"But I was personally requested..." Marian opened the door to see Robert's poor attempt at trying to get into the room.

75

"Robert, please come in." Gisbourne had no choice but to step aside. Marian watched him for a moment, instantly suspicious of why he was so adamant that Robert should not look at the body. As soon as Robert was inside, Marian slammed the door, glancing over at Alan apologetically.

"Why did you ask for me? I am no expert at investigating deaths."

"Shh," Marian whispered, to make sure Gisbourne could not eavesdrop. "Please Robert. I cannot trust anyone else with this. I believe foul play killed Walt... the Sheriff." Marian could not bring herself to say his name. She still did not truly believe he could be dead, even though she could obviously see he was. She just could not process it.

Robert started to examine Walter, looking at his body for any signs of foul play.

Marian watched him anxiously.

"There is no sign of a struggle and no obvious wound. Although..."

"What is it?"

"There is a smell..." He went close to the Sheriff's face and with his fingers he carefully opened his mouth.

At that moment, the door swung open, slamming into the wall behind it, disturbing the peace of the dead. Robert moved away from the Sheriff instantly. A maid rushed in and shut the door using her back, holding it there as though someone might break through it.

"What is going on?" Marian demanded.

"I...I..." The maid was out of breath. She looked at Robert and sighed with relief. "I found him dead but there was nothing I could do. I know something is wrong. It felt odd last night, but I do not question those above me. Sir Guy of Gisbourne asked me to give an urgent letter to his messenger and he would take the Sheriff's meal in to save me the trouble. I was sure the Sheriff was looking better yesterday. Then suddenly he was dead!" Marian took a few moments to process all this information; the maid had told her story so fast it was hard for Marian to follow.

"How did you get in here? Was Gisbourne not outside?"

"Well, I kind of told him a lie. I may have said I saw someone trying to steal his horse and carriage..." she said with a mischievous smile.

Now was not the time for playing around, Marian frowned. She looked at Robert expectantly. He looked from the maid to Marian and gave a surprised 'oh', having been distracted by the easily amused maid. Marian watched as he sniffed near the Sheriff's mouth.

"I am no expert at such things but I have encountered this scent before on another who died very shortly after. I could not explain what was wrong with her before she died, but now I know that smell. It must be some sort of poison. It does not have much of a taste, which is why it is such a clever way to kill discreetly. But the smell is definitely potent, it must have been a strong dose as the whole room smells off. Yes, I am sure it was poison."

Gisbourne. He had been the last one to access the room and he must have believed he had disposed of all the evidence. She had never known bloodthirst like it. She focused all her energy on rage against this cowardly animal that could not even kill a man fairly.

Marian decided to stay at the castle that night, as someone had to keep an eye on Gisbourne. She was to watch him and confront him when the time was right. She slept alone in a guest room, with Alan sleeping close by in another room. Marian had requested he stay close to her, and not in the servants' quarters, making the excuse that she felt safer and more comfortable with him close by – and in a way, that was the truth. She did not know what else Gisbourne might be capable of, or who might be his next target.

She was alone in the room. She did not want to be, but she had little choice. Now was not a good time to be alone to her thoughts. They tended to have a habit of making everything worse for herself.

Am I not destined for happiness? Is this my life now? Running from shadows that will do anything to get what they want? Marian did not sleep well that night. Whenever she started to drift off, she would force herself awake over fear of what her nightmares might bring.

The early morning sun made Marian's room explode into colour. She was exhausted but her mind had finally cleared. Today she would get justice for Walter's death. Then she would be able to grieve properly. Overnight she had devised a plan. She would expose Gisbourne's weakness, which she hoped was still his love for her, if she could call it that. He had, after all, wanted to support her grief. And she would let him.

Before the castle awoke, Marian snuck around the corridor until she was outside Gisbourne's room. It felt wrong, at this time, waiting outside a man's private chamber. She felt like a naughty child spying on someone. *I will avenge Walter's death. This is for Walter*, she had to remind herself.

She knocked.

The door seemed to open excruciatingly slowly, but when he finally peered around, he was caught unawares; she could tell by his surprised expression. Marian wanted to laugh at the absurdity but did not dare.

"Marian? What brings you here at this time? Do you need me?" He looked deeply into her eyes, searching for some kind of affection. *He wants me to need him. He cannot know me at all. Oh well, if that is what he wants…*

"I just… I feel so alone. I know you are there for me, always." For effect, Marian leant in close.

He kissed her hard and fast. Marian closed her eyes, not out of love but pure disgust. She shut her eyes so tightly she could see stars behind her eyelids. She felt physically sick, kissing the man who had just murdered the person she loved most. Marian tried to make it feel to him like this was real. She ran her hands up and down his body and struck gold. On a chain around his neck was a vial containing the poison, Marian could only hope. He would not be able to resist taking it with him in case he had use for it. She kissed him harder and at the same time yanked the chain, pulling it off into her hand. She instantly let go of Gisbourne, mumbling.

"I am sorry. I cannot do this. I am in mourning. I should not be…" She ran as fast as her legs would take her. It was so much easier than she had thought possible. As Marian ran past Alan's door, she heard footsteps coming up behind her, just like her nightmares. Marian stopped and turned around. Several guards surrounded her. She did not have a plan for this. She should have expected it; Gisbourne had full command of the guards. She heard a door creak open, and a half-dressed Alan walked out. Before he even opened his mouth to speak, guards seized him and took him away.

"Where are you taking him?" Marian demanded. "We have done nothing wrong! Did that kiss mean nothing to you?" She glared directly at Gisbourne, trying to look like a silly little girl – innocent and naïve.

"Really, Marian? I was warned about you. He told me you were trouble, but I would not listen. You betrayed me."

"Well you betrayed Nottingham. You betrayed our Sheriff. You murdered Walter and I have proof." She held the vial out so the guards could see it. She thought some of them might at least back down, but nobody so much as flinched. Gisbourne had too much hold over them.

"What evidence? The rightful Sheriff has declared you to be a liar and traitor. No one will ever believe what comes out of your mouth again."

"Rightful? This was your plan all along? You had a new Sheriff lined up ready to take over. You just needed to kill off the old one." Marian had never been so revolted at someone in her entire life, and she had met some disturbing creatures. "We have not even buried the old Sheriff yet. Walter is still in his bed."

"You will find he has disappeared. How unfortunate. No funeral ceremony can take place now, such a shame. I suspect some sort of witchcraft was involved. Maybe they will brand you a witch and drown you." Tears rolled down Marian's cheeks and she could do nothing to stop them flowing. Before she could react, the vial was back in Gisbourne's hands. "I think the Sheriff would like to see her. Take her to the hall."

Chapter 14

The guards escorted Marian to the Great Hall. From what Gisbourne had suggested, it sounded like the new Sheriff had already been appointed, whoever he was. Somehow, this new Sheriff must know her as Gisbourne had said he warned him about her. But not many people did know her, she had made sure of it. That unsettling feeling in the pit of her stomach was worsening into pain. How could a new Sheriff have been assigned so fast? Then everything clicked together. Gisbourne must have murdered Walter under the new Sheriff's instruction. A man with such authority must be very powerful indeed, she realised, and Marian started to fear who could be sitting in Walter's throne. She did not know what awaited her. She was only certain of one thing: it would not be good.

Marian was almost at the door now. The guards surrounding her all stopped at once, and she almost fell into the ones in front of her. One of the guards searched her carefully. She was surprised Gisbourne had not wanted the honour himself, to be able to get close to her. Marian tried to act normal, and she closed her eyes praying they would not find the dagger hidden in a fastening on her dress. At that thought, she felt a pull on her dress and the dagger fell out. She noticed Gisbourne raise an eyebrow in surprise before his face returned to its usual unreadable blankness.

She hoped Alan was alright. They could not have any evidence that he was involved in any criminal activity, and Gisbourne did not know he was an outlaw. She should have told Alan her plans, perhaps it would have turned out differently, or maybe it was best he did not know, as now he would not need to fake his innocence. Marian hoped that he believed in God, so that he might know Heaven was there to welcome him. In a way, Marian wished she carried the belief, as it would make death so much easier to understand and saying goodbye would not be forever. In God's eyes, she would be able to see Walter again one day, but she could not bring herself to believe in such nonsense.

The doors opened in front of her, and she was pushed inside. Marian jumped as the doors closed behind her with a mighty slam. She turned back towards the doors. All the guards were stationed outside the doors. She would not even have a witness for whatever was about to happen.

"Did you think we would be so stupid to give you an exit. All my men are posted at every window, every door you could possibly try to escape from. Give up." Of course Gisbourne was enjoying this, he was the sort of person who revelled in seeing others helpless and afraid.

Gisbourne walked up to the Sheriff's chair. She tried to see who it might be, but he had a cloak over his head. Gisbourne leant into the Sheriff and whispered something, then stepped back. The Sheriff stood and faced Marian, walking part way across the hall, down his steps to be level with her. There was still a distance between them, but she would be able to see his face if only he removed his hood. He pulled back his hood suddenly, like he knew what she was thinking. And…

#

Alan was dragged down the cold gaol steps, the back of his legs hitting the stone floor hard. He could not get his head around what was happening. He had heard a commotion outside his room, gotten out of bed and opened his door, and there had been Marian. As soon as he had seen her, he heard Gisbourne bark orders and he was dragged away from her. He had not had time to even ask what was going on. His only concern was for Marian. What had she done to Gisbourne? He had a dangerous look in his eyes, and Alan feared for Marian's life more than he thought possible.

The guards had stopped dragging him and he took a moment to compose himself. The jailer unlocked a cell and pushed Alan inside. He locked the door again with a big clunk.

Alan slumped against a wall.

He would probably die, and he deserved it. His crimes were not severe, but he had hurt a lot of people. As an outlaw, Alan had killed many men, most of which were dangerous murderers who lurked in the forest and he had no choice with those men. But now he questioned the necessity. He might have been able to save some of them, swayed them to be better people, or he could have at least tried. He had mercilessly killed them to stop the threat but had not thought about whether they might have families. Alan had blood on his hands, and he deserved to suffer for it.

He resigned himself to death. He would face it head on and without fear. He prayed silently for Marian's survival, rather than his own. In this moment, he realised he loved Marian. Not familial love, but he was in love with her. He decided that the last person he would see in his mind's eye when he died, would be her. She was his salvation, his angel.

#

Marian's world came crashing down. It resembled the nightmares she had suffered every night since that fateful day. She was looking into the eyes of the devil. Possessed, unable to move, she could do nothing but stare in horror. *This is not just a bad dream. This is real.*

Uncle.

Gisbourne was suddenly beside Marian, pushing her forward, delicately at first, but when she failed to respond, he shoved her forcefully and she fell to the ground with a thud. Somehow it brought her back to reality and she realised she needed to get away. She was breathless and her heart pounded. She could not feel the pain of being pushed to the floor.

She could not feel the pain of losing Walter. All she knew was fear.

She forgot her training, stood and ran towards the door as fast as her legs would allow her. But before she could reach it, Gisbourne pulled her back with such force she flew across the room, sending her closer to her uncle than she had been before. Marian scrambled away from him, but Gisbourne had already caught up to her, using all his strength to pull her up onto her feet, holding her arms so tightly she was sure his nails pierced her skin. Gisbourne pushed her into one of the chairs and used rope to hold her in place. The moment she sat down, she gave up. This was the end, and she knew it. She was fed up of running away.

Anyway, she had no choice now. That plan had failed her.

"How?" she breathed, the last of her energy ebbing. She had not meant to say it aloud but she could not process her thoughts clearly. Her uncle had been turned away from her, but when he heard her speak, he snapped towards her. Marian trembled under the intensity of his gaze. He could see right through her. Any attempt at distracting him would be useless.

"Oh, how I have missed your wailing, babyish little voice. I have often thought of seeing you again. What I would do to you; my revenge. I bet you thought it impossible, that I could really be here. Do not insult my intelligence. It has not taken me this long to find you. I have known you were here for some time now. Did you like my little gift to you?" He smiled, a devious, scheming grin than sent chills down her spine. "Gisbourne is a beauty. We go way back. In fact, I made him what he is today. Like mine, his target has always been you. You never even saw it coming, did you? I have waited so long for this moment. But why rush? We have all the time in the world. Have a drink, Mary." He said her name slowly, just like how he used to say it; the voice that haunted her dreams was now real. Her body shook uncontrollably.

Marian wanted to say something, anything. Her mouth opened ready to speak, but nothing came out. Even her voice had given up on her. Her thoughts returned to Alan. She was guilty of betraying him. She wished she had confided in him, as now she had sentenced him to death for no reason. There was no way to save him now. She had only thought about herself and now her friend would die because of her. Her uncle would kill Alan without a thought.

"Worried about your friend, little Mary? Do not worry; his death will be quick, unlike yours. You will see him again shortly." He could read each and every thought. There was no escape.

Marian's fear turned to fury in an instant. She had to survive. She could not let Alan suffer for what she had done. He had nothing to do with this. She squirmed, trying to free herself from the rope, some unknown force giving her energy to go on, but it was no use.

"Gisbourne, pour Marian a glass of your *special* wine. Not too strong, women are too weak to stomach much of the stuff." Marian knew exactly what her uncle was asking of Gisbourne. She watched as he poured a glass of wine for the Sheriff and another for her. He opened the vial which was back around his neck and let a couple of drops fall into her glass. He gave the Sheriff his glass and then started towards Marian.

Marian closed her mouth tight, glaring at Gisbourne with manic rage. He yanked her head back and in the shock of it she opened her mouth and before she could close it again, he was pouring the liquid down her throat. She squirmed and wriggled as much as she could, some of the contents of the glass spilling onto her dress. She choked as she tried to stop the flow, until there was no wine left. Marian tried to gag but nothing came up. This was the end.

But she felt no different. She did not know the effect poison was supposed to make, only that it would result in death, the same fate as Walter had suffered. She hoped his death had been quick and painless, but she knew hers would not be so easy. She expected some sort of pain, but she felt alive and fine. She smiled, somehow it was not working.

Then her uncle smiled back at her, his eyes glowing with amusement. "Do not be so smug. The poison will work in due course. It was a smaller amount than we gave poor Walter. Who knows how long you will last? I wonder how long it will take you to figure out whether it is real or not. Now for a little trip down memory lane. Mary, before you go off on whatever meaningless things you want to do before you die, I want to take you somewhere I know you will love." He turned to Gisbourne. "Get the guards to escort Mary to the carriage. I will meet you in a few moments. First I must address my people."

#

Alan shivered on the damp floor and after attempting to get comfortable, he gave up. He stood and began to pace his cell, unable to bear the silence. He heard a shuffle a little way away, and a woman appeared.

"Hi there, my name is Emma. I am Beatrice's friend. She asked me to keep an eye on you and Marian while you are at the castle. You have gotten yourself into a bit of bother there. I am sorry but there is not much I can do. Why are you in here?"

"I do not know. I think Marian hatched a plan and got caught. Do you know what has happened to her? Is she alright?" Alan was glad for some company and he remembered Beatrice telling them Emma could be trusted. It was useful to have someone on the inside, even more so now.

"She is alive, that is all I know. Gisbourne took her to see the new Sheriff, and he sounds horrid."

"What? We have a new Sheriff already? What happened to a procession for Walter first?"

"Gisbourne claimed the body vanished; something to do with witchcraft to scare the people out of questioning it. In fact, I had better go. The new Sheriff is making his first address to the people. I will come back later." She passed him a piece of bread through the bars of the cell and rushed off, the sound of her footsteps echoing as she got further away until there was silence once more.

At least Marian was alive. He hoped she had enough friends who would help her out of whatever situation she was in. He had done his best to keep her safe, but it was not good enough. He had failed in his promise to protect her, and now he would die for it.

Chapter 15

"My people. You do not know me yet, but soon you shall grow to be loyal. I am the High Sheriff of Nottinghamshire, Derbyshire and the Royal Forests. I plan to make your home the centre of England. I am backed by many powerful allies and I will achieve their wishes by any means. I hope I make this clear to you all. From now on I am in charge. I do not like to be challenged, take this as a warning.

"Now, I have some important business to attend to. I expect you to work harder than you have ever worked before. The King is not pleased with your laziness and lack of taxes. There will be a renewed presence of guards throughout the city to ensure standards are met. Rest assured I will be made aware of any discrepancies and there shall be consequences."

Emma stared in horror at the man who stood at the top of the steps leading to the castle, surrounded by the fiercest looking guards. He was not a tall man, but he wore such expensive clothes that made him look all the more terrifying. He had thinning hair showing his age, but his eyes were focused, and he meant business. Emma's heart stammered in her chest. She thought her life was already tough enough, her son was all she had left, and she could barely provide for the both of them as it was. She was going to face an even tougher life ahead.

#

Marian was escorted out the back of the castle, to avoid the gathering of people waiting to hear from the new High Sheriff. *At least,* she thought to herself, *I have a few moments without Gisbourne and uncle. My last seconds of freedom – use it wisely.*

Marian slowed, and the guards slowed with her, oddly not trying to rush her. She searched the grounds for someone she recognised. Several maids were running around, with tasks to prepare for the new Sheriff. Marian caught the eye of someone in the shadows. He stepped out and she recognised Tuck. He looked at her quizzically. Marian shook her head, warding him off trying to help her. It was more important to save Alan – he was innocent in the situation and should not be punished for what she had done. She looked towards the castle, hoping Tuck would understand. As usual, he knew exactly what she meant.

Marian guessed Tuck had heard rumours about her and a young man being imprisoned. He winked at Marian and wandered over to a guard posted at the servants' entrance she and her entourage of guards had just passed through. Marian had a renewed admiration for Tuck. Even though most people cast him aside as little more than a drunk, Marian saw his true talent. He was cunning and clever, and a great ally to have. She slowed down even more to listen to what he had to say to the guard. She heard him clear his throat, and sounding like the religious symbol she once knew him as, he spoke:

"I am here to receive the prisoner's last confessions before execution."

"I have heard nothing of the sort."

"Do you dare defy God's wishes?"

Marian listened, with an inward sigh of relief, as the gates opened for Tuck to enter.

She felt at peace, knowing that Alan would be safe.

#

Tuck entered the castle with a new sense of purpose. He felt this was the right thing to do. Earlier in the tavern he had heard a servant talking about Marian, claiming to have seen her being escorted by guards and she had looked in trouble. A young man had also been imprisoned in the gaol. When Marian had looked towards the castle, he knew she meant for him to rescue the young man and not herself. She would refuse help if he tried to assist her in escaping and it was a little too adventurous for a drunk like himself. He had not had any ale for two days as he had felt a big change in the locals and could feel something was about to happen.

He sometimes had premonitions about these sorts of things. Tuck often wondered if it was God's will that gave him this ability, but could not be certain. He had not felt much of a presence in God for a long time. He raised the hood of his cloak over his head and moved his hands to a praying position as he walked the corridors of the castle. He had been in the castle on a couple of occasions when he used to be a friar, but since he left the church, he had not set foot inside the castle; there had simply been no reason.

Now he walked the castle as a fraud; a non-believer frowned upon by the people but many in the castle would not recognise him. The sorts of people who frequented the tavern and noticed him were not the type you would find in a castle like this, only those who did not want to be recognised; Guy of Gisbourne, for instance.

Finally Tuck found the stairs down to the gaol. At the bottom stood a locked gate that one of the two guards positioned in front of it would possess the key to.

When Walter had been in charge, Tuck had rarely seen the castle gaol used, as most offences were seen to in the Shire Hall, where trials would take place fairly. Those who committed crimes were kept in dungeons well below street level, carved into the caves under the Hall, awaiting trial. Walter had always ensured prisoners did not spend long in there until their trials. Tuck had been down a few times and though the caves were very beautiful in themselves, it was a very lonely place, so far underground. He had a lot of respect for Walter's equality to criminals, unlike most other figures of power who loved a good hanging, and even the smallest offence would warrant the most severe punishment in most counties.

"God has granted me passage into these chambers to receive the last wishes of the prisoners," Tuck said to the guards. He walked forward until the guards stiffened and readied their weapons. Tuck stopped right in front of both guards and started to feel for a chain around his neck he had not touched for years, that had sat limp against his chest under his robes, unmoving but still there all the same. He kissed the cross and made a silent prayer to God that if he were there, he would absolve the sins he was about to commit. He dropped the chain back to his chest and in one smooth motion pulled out two concealed daggers from his robes and plunged them into the necks of the two guards simultaneously.

In an instant, he pulled the daggers back out and the men dropped to the ground, almost silently, only the sound of the armour clinking on the stone floor. He found the keys dangling off one of the guards' belts and equipped himself with the sword and belt attached to it too, just in case. Tuck had gained a belly since he started drinking and he had to loosen the belt a lot to fit it around his robes.

He followed the winding path in darkness and heard whimpers as he passed cells. He could smell rotting flesh and every now and then he would step in something slick on the floor; he did not want to know what it was. Peering into a few cells he noticed bodies curled up in corners, hunched and frail – it was clear they had been here a long time. Had this all been Gisbourne's doing? Walter would never have treated his people in such a horrid manner. Had Walter really lost all power when Gisbourne arrived in town? Tuck felt a pang of guilt for these men, but he could not save them all, not yet anyway. Many of them could be guilty themselves, he told himself, but they did not deserve this ill-treatment.

Tuck froze as he heard scuffling ahead. A young woman sat in front of one of the gaol cells. When he was certain she was not a threat, he proceeded, rattling the keys so as not to make her jump. She turned around, surprised and stared up to him.

"Who are you?" she asked, bewildered.

"My name is Friar Tuck. Who, might I ask, are you?" "Tuck?" A small voice came from inside the cell.

"That is my name." Tuck pronounced, squinting to see into the cell.

"You are Marian's friend," the man spoke more cheerfully.

"You are Marian's friend also, I presume. Alan?"

"Aye. What are you doing here? Do you bring news of Marian?" He shuffled forward and rested his head against the metal of the gate. Up close, Alan was quite handsome. He could see why Marian kept him around.

"Marian is being escorted out of the castle. Her request was for me to get you out."

"A friar? How can you, a man of God, help me escape? Is that not against your rules?"

"I make my own rules and I decide for myself what is right and what is wrong. Do not question it or I will leave you here and deny what could be Marian's last request."

Emma stood suddenly. "No. It cannot be her last request. We must help her!"

"First let me get you out." Tuck tried several keys before the right one fit into the lock.

"Now what shall I do? I can get Beatrice to help," Emma suggested.

"Beatrice? Oh, Marian's maid. Yes, go to her and tell her we are going to help Marian, to put her mind at ease. I have heard how much she fusses over Marian. In fact, Marian often comes to me for relief from her constant jabbering!" Tuck laughed at his quip.

"No time for this, we need to get going," Alan said urgently.

"Let us get you out of here quickly. Then you can go find your outlaw friends to assist us. We cannot do this alone. Emma, run ahead and cause a distraction – fall in front of some guards and they will come rushing to your aid." Emma looked at him scornfully, then winked and ran off.

Tuck and Alan waited a few moments then ran faster than Tuck had ever thought possible with his belly. He enjoyed the thrill and did not even feel guilty about it. He was free.

#

The carriage journey was long and harsh. It seemed to take an eternity, travelling at the edge of the woods. Marian guessed they did not want to come across any trouble in the forest, so instead took the safer, longer route to wherever they were going. She looked out the window for the entirety of the journey, perhaps the last time she would see the world in all its beauty. She sensed Gisbourne watching her but refused to acknowledge him. Finally, the carriage turned and started into the forest.

Marian glimpsed a face hiding in the shadows. She blinked, and then it was gone. It must have been her imagination. Walter had often spoken of his love for travelling. He had always promised one day he would see everything. He never got the chance. He used to tell her stories of some of his journeys to beautiful, mysterious places. She had always presumed it was his way of comforting her, like a bedtime story to a young child. *Perhaps*, Marian thought, *there is a place after death*. Even though she did not believe in religion, which everyone – even Walter – had frowned upon, she held on to the idea that there was some type of heaven, as it was the only comfort she could think of for herself.

Eventually the carriage came to a standstill and the door opened. The Sheriff stepped out first, followed by Gisbourne, who – ever the gentleman – helped her down. She would have jumped down herself and refused his help, but it would have been hard with her hands bound together under the Sheriff's orders. He knew she would otherwise try to escape.

Marian looked around, at first confused as to why they had brought her into a random part of the forest. *Are they going to execute me away from prying eyes?* Marian did not think so; her uncle's methods were always much crueller and theatrical. Gisbourne tapped on the carriage and the driver moved out of the way, revealing before her the ruins of a house. It looked like it had burned down a long time ago, with overgrown shrubs protruding out of the wreckage. Something in the back of her mind pulsed with familiarity. She was blocking a memory that would not reveal itself.

"Perhaps you have forgotten, but this used to be my home, our home. What happened, you ask? Well the nine servants would say *you* happened. The day they helped you escape was the day I burned this dump to the ground, all of them locked inside. They did not have a chance. Their charred remains are probably around here somewhere..." He carried on, but there was a high-pitched ringing in Marian's head that drowned out the rest of the world.

#

Tuck followed Alan through the forest to find a messenger who could report back to Alan's old gang. On the way, Alan told Tuck stories of his life as an outlaw and it did appeal to him. The fresh air and the liberty of living in the forest brought to mind a feeling of great relief.

Tuck had lived a sheltered life in his youth. His parents believed God had come to them both in a dream and told them Tuck was to become a religious symbol. When he was only six years old, his parents had taken him to church to become a monk. He had found it very tough with strict rules. He found it hard in different ways than most others. They all struggled with the vow of chastity, but Tuck had not cared about sexual desire at his youthful age. Many of the other novices he had grown up with were much older than him and they had been surrounded by those who had sexual relationships. It was the life of solitude that irritated him, as he had always wanted a life of freedom, to see the world. When he finally took his vows, friars were becoming commonplace, and it appealed greatly to him. It would give him the freedom to explore while being able to spread the word of God. His request was accepted, and he was released into the world.

He had not realised how cruel the world was, however, as he soon saw disease that killed, innocents being hung for petty crimes, and powerful men who did not take care of their people. He missed the sheltered life of a monk but knew he could make the world a better place by giving the people belief and hope.

Tuck rarely reminisced about his life before drink. He had not technically broken any vows, but it had become an addiction. He did not understand why God made him like this and gave up completely. Why would God create a world with so many temptations? That was when his belief left him, and he gave in to the desire of drink.

As Alan and Tuck walked, Tuck had his first vision in years. A female leader surrounded by many followers, all looking to her for hope. This was part of his future and God had found him again. He had not been sober for a very long time and he felt free for the first time in his entire life. He belonged here, fighting injustice. It was his calling.

It did not take too long to reach the messenger, but by the time they arrived, Tuck was starting to feel the effects of a day of running and regretted putting on all this extra weight. He was not as fit as he used to be, and it was holding him back.

They reached a small clearing and Alan had been true to his word. A hooded man leant against a tree, appearing to be asleep. However, as they entered the clearing, the man stood upright, surprising Tuck enough to take a step back. But Alan simply stood in front of the man, unmoving.

"Robin?" Alan asked.

"What is wrong?" the man demanded.

"Why are you here? Where is the messenger?"

"Do you not want me here?"

"No. I mean yes I do want you here. It is Marian. She is in trouble and I am going to rescue her with or without your help."

#

Robin had tried with all his might to stay away from Nottingham, but he could not help himself. Something attracted him to it, maybe his youthful past here, or perhaps it was Marian. He could not understand the impulse but no matter how hard he tried to distract himself, he could not stop thinking about it. He had resorted to going to one of his messengers closer to Nottingham and asking him to gather information about the people and especially Gisbourne, to find out what he was planning. Now it seemed Marian was caught up in all of this as well and he could not leave her to her fate.

Robin gathered the men camped nearby and some of his scouts that were positioned along the route and together they tracked the carriage carrying Marian southwards of Nottingham. By the time they gathered everyone within range, there were 17 including Robin, Alan and Tuck. Robin took an instant liking to

Tuck and found him fascinating. Talking to him about life as a drunken friar was a good distraction from his dark thoughts.

#

Marian could no longer breathe. Her throat tightened and tears streamed down her face. Her past clung to her, weighing her down. *It is my fault. All of it. Meggy and all the other innocents died because of me. They all died. I had not even given them a thought since I left them behind.*

Marian's knees gave way. Her whole life had been a lie she had told herself. She had thought herself the victim and never had a second thought for those who helped her escape. She was numb. *I do not deserve to live. I am worse than my uncle.* The guilt was too much to carry; it was suffocating her.

In the distance, she could faintly hear voices. Somehow her hands were not bound anymore. She did not care if she died now, it would be a release from the torment. She was broken; a shell of a person. *I am lost.*

Chapter 16

Robin heard a noise ahead and motioned for the men to stop. They were under the cover of trees and could easily hide, though he doubted Tuck could go on much further. Tuck had slowed to a pace behind everyone else and when Robin and his men stopped, it took a few moments for Tuck to catch up with them.

"Come, Gisbourne. Let us leave her to her fate." Robin did not recognise the voice and he looked to Tuck.

"The Sheriff," Tuck wheezed next to him, trying to catch his breath.

The mention of Gisbourne sent a shiver down Robin's spine and he was poised to strike and kill him. He felt a hand on his shoulder and turned to see Alan there.

"We have come to help Marian, not to seek revenge on Gisbourne. That can wait. Besides, we do not have enough men to attack. Perhaps Gisbourne will be useful to us yet. He has a vendetta against Arthur, it could one day play to our advantage," Alan whispered to him.

"It is true," Tuck agreed breathlessly. "The Sheriff and Gisbourne are leaving. We wait until they pass then continue on to Marian."

"Good idea Friar," Robin agreed. He noticed Tuck flinch at the word friar as though he did not deserve the title. "You have done a great service by freeing Alan."

"I did it for Marian," he replied instinctively.

They all watched in silence as Gisbourne and the Sheriff left in their carriage, guards surrounding them, urging the horses onwards and back to Nottingham. As soon as the carriage was out of sight, slowly and carefully they walked into the clearing, just in case it was a trap. Robin noticed Marian knelt on the ground, her white dress dirty and stained and her hair cascading down her back. He started towards her, some invisible force spurring him on, but he stopped himself before he could reach her; he could not show weakness in front of his men.

However, he could not stop his heart wrenching, as he turned to Alan and motioned for him to approach her instead.

#

Slowly Marian's senses returned to her. Her ears stopped ringing and she could hear footsteps approaching from behind. She waited for the blow that would kill her. Perhaps her uncle really was a coward, or maybe he had left Gisbourne to finish her off. She would welcome death. At this point it would be a mercy. *I am a monster, a murderer.* Someone was blocking her view, but all she could do was stare at the ruins, a reminder of who she really was. The person was talking but she could not seem to focus on what they were saying.

Robin's voice broke through the barrier and she was suddenly aware of the scene around her.

"Is she alright?" He sounded desperate, worried. He should not care about her; she did not deserve any help.

A hand on her shoulder, she flinched, waiting for the pain to come. But nothing happened. Slowly the world came back into focus. Alan was in front of her, his worried eyes searching her face for something. "Did they hurt you?"

Tears streamed down her face, her heart shrivelling inside her. A dead weight with no meaning. She was not the person she had thought herself to be. She was worse than her uncle, worse than Gisbourne. She had no soul, no care for those she had left behind, until now.

"Robin, please try," she heard Alan plead as he walked away. She should be left to herself. She did not want witnesses. She tried to focus on the voices behind her.

"No. I just… she knows you," Robin replied.

"But you have a past, perhaps you can bring her back. I cannot get through to her," he begged.

"You do not understand…" Robin tried.

Someone was in front of her again, but her eyes had blurred from the tears.

"Marian, it is me, Robin. Please come back to us. We are worried about you."

"I deserve nothing. Leave me here." Marian did not mean to say such a thing, but she was not herself. She did not know who she was anymore. She could not concentrate on Robin. He did care after all, but he should not. She did not deserve these men to care about her.

"Thank you for sending Tuck in. You saved Alan's life," Robin said, trying to sound positive. Marian did not deserve the gratitude of anyone. She had blood on her hands.

I saved no one. I caused their deaths. These people should be running from me, not trying to help me.

Marian could sense Robin's tension increase. She was beyond the point of help. Even if she could be helped, she did not want it. He spoke, breaking the unearthly silence where once screams of terror had rung out.

"It is getting dark. We need to get out of here. There is a cave a couple of hours walk from here." Ever the leader, Robin took command. He walked away.

Marian was ready for them to leave her there, but she knew Alan would not allow it.

"Can you walk?" Alan asked kindly, beside her. Marian did not dare to answer because truthfully, she did not know if she could move at all, let alone walk. Without a word, Tuck appeared and offered her a hand while Alan steadied her. Marian followed behind everyone else, unsure how she was putting one foot in front of another. *Selfish; why am I doing this? I should have stayed behind. It would only be right to die in the same place as my victims.*

Alan and Tuck were close by, watching her. She still could not bring herself to speak; she did not know what she would say anyway. Alan should not be worrying about her. Marian looked ahead of her the whole time, and for a moment she noticed Robin looking towards her. His face obscured into the child she once knew him as. A little girl ran past Marian. She stared in disbelief as she recognised herself from the first time she met Robin Hood, the boy who gave her hope. Her back burned with the memory of what happened next, and she stopped, trying to catch her breath. She looked down at herself. Marian was no longer that little girl. The nightmares that haunted her sleep were now haunting her consciousness. Past and present blurred into one and she could no longer remember which was real. She tried to battle against it, putting one foot in front of the other. Walking through the pain of memories, flashes of her younger self ran past, terrified. A dress ripping as she ran past trees. That little girl would never give up. Who had she become? A part of her wanted to keep going; her life had to be worth something. There was a reason she was still alive.

The rest of the outlaws were far ahead and barely visible in the distance. Marian stopped suddenly in the middle of a road. She recognised it instantly. She watched as her memory played out in front of her. Mary ran across the road, tripping over. She heard a voice in her head, *uncle*. She could not breathe. She felt something wet on her face, but she was not crying; she had a fever. Marian closed her eyes and tried to focus. Footsteps behind her and she lurched forward, losing her balance.

Then Alan was there holding her steady.

"Marian, what is wrong? Please tell me. You are acting strange."

"Everything is wrong. I am wrong."

"Perhaps I should take you home. What did Gisbourne and that new Sheriff do? You can trust me."

"But you should not trust me. I cannot go home." She panicked. "You cannot take me home. It is a lie. I do not remember my home. Nottingham was a lie. Those ruins are not home. Where is my home?" *Something is happening to me – poison.* "I killed them all. That was me." She backed away from Alan. "Stay away from me. I will kill you too." Marian closed her eyes. Pain pulsed through her body. She gritted her teeth, willing the pain away.

"Marian?"

She opened her eyes, looking directly at Tuck. "Get away!" Her uncle stood in front of her. "Why are you here? I am already dying. Changed your mind? Want to do it yourself? Go ahead. This is my punishment."

Robin blocked her view of him. "Marian. It is me, Robin. Remember? We go way back." He moved closer, dropping his weapons, holding his hands out to her. "Marian, look at me, focus on me."

Robin Hood. He is a friend. "It hurts."

"What is wrong? I can help. Remember. We promised, Marian."

"I think…my uncle… poisoned me." She gasped, trying desperately to tell him what had happened. She was scared of death, too weak to put on a brave face. She took everything back; she did not want to die. Wheezing for air, pain gripped her. Her legs gave way and Robin was beside her.

"Bring me the cart we passed a little way back. I know someone who can help. We will have to travel in dark. The rest of you gather supplies and weapons. We leave soon." His voice faded as did the world around her. She let the darkness consume her.

Chapter 17

Alan had never felt so utterly useless. Watching Marian suffer like that reminded him of his parents being killed in front of him, unable to do anything but watch as the inevitable happened. He was surprised how Robin had acted so human and vulnerable for the first time he had ever witnessed. That glimpse of emotion, of love? Robin did feel something for Marian. He just did not understand why he supressed it so much. What Alan would give for Marian to choose him over Robin, but she was too good for him, although Robin was no better. Perhaps he did stand a chance. He did not owe Robin anything. But he could be a friend to Robin, if only he would show more of his humanity. He forced himself away from these thoughts as his attention returned to whether Marian would survive. *She could not just die, surely not?*

He tried to piece together the scene. It was like Marian was trying to tell them something, to confide in him, but in her state, she had mixed everything together, making it impossible for him to understand. She had said something about an uncle, but that must have been her fever talking. All he knew was that she had been poisoned, by Gisbourne's hand no doubt. If he lost Marian, he vowed to himself he would seek justice and kill Gisbourne, or he would die trying.

Alan walked beside the cart which carried Marian the whole journey. Tuck sat on the cart, resting his tired legs. Alan watched over Marian like a guardian angel and was relieved to have the friar's company.

Travelling at night was disconcerting, but Robin must know the route very well. Alan himself had never met the mysterious healer Grishelda, but he had heard stories from the other outlaws. Grishelda had a long history with Robin's family. Alan had also heard, however, that Robin had not seen Grishelda since Connor had died. Robin had gone to her several times, pleading for a cure for Connor, but she had refused unless he came to her.

Despite Robin's attempts, Connor had refused help, claiming he was still fit to lead; Connor had too much pride, but he had been a good leader.

A noise from the cart and Marian stirred. She clutched her stomach in agony and Alan winced, wanting to help her, but the only way to help was to get her to Grishelda as fast as possible. Tuck hushed her calmly and turned his head to Alan, questioning.

"Not far," Alan answered to the unspoken question on Tuck's lips. Tuck offered a hand for her to hold on to. She took it and tried to speak but she fell unconscious from the pain. Alan was certain Marian was trying to tell them something, but he had to push it to the back of his mind. He had to focus on saving her first.

After hours of walking, finally they arrived. The men gathered around the cart, and Tuck still held Marian's hand, to Alan's comfort. Tuck was a kindly man, and he was glad he was there for Marian. Alan looked down at her. She was dreaming about something. He had watched her sleep before, and he knew the nightmares were real for her, but this was different. Usually she would wake up after a few minutes of a nightmare. This time he watched as she became more and more fearful, fitting, feverish. He could almost see the poison pulsing through her veins. He was forced to look away when Robin spoke.

"Alan, carry Marian. The rest of you stay outside, in the shadows. I do not want Grishelda to feel overpowered. I will be out shortly. Make camp, it will be light soon. Then you can rest."

Alan picked Marian up like a baby; she was so precious. She stirred slightly in the shift of weight but did not wake. She was slick with sweat and murmuring to herself. He followed Robin to the door, where he knocked three times, an unspoken code. He waited a few seconds then knocked again, more urgent this time. Alan had a sickening thought that she might not be in or might not want to help. They were in the middle of the forest; there was no one else who could help Marian.

The door creaked open, and a grubby old woman stood, with her arms crossed. Her eyes glared into Robin's like daggers, if looks could kill. Then her eyes brightened, and she smiled, revealing her blackened teeth. Alan wondered in amazement at how Robin and his family had ever met such a strange creature.

"I need your help," Robin told her. At that, Grishelda looked over to Alan and then at Marian and she ushered them in quickly. Tuck tried to enter behind them, but she gave him a wary look and he stood back. Grishelda glanced suspiciously into the forest before shutting the door behind them.

With one clean swoop, Grishelda pushed everything off the table and gestured for Alan to place Marian on it. He did so without hesitation, confused and fascinated by her oddness.

"I do not have all day!" Alan was glad to no longer be carrying Marian or he might have dropped her from the sharpness of Grishelda's tongue.

"She was poisoned, that is all I know. Can you help? Please say you can help?" Alan stared at Robin, unbelieving of the emotion he was witnessing. He sounded so desperate, so unlike himself. He noticed Grishelda looking at Robin quizzically as well. She snapped out of it straight away and went about examining Marian.

For such an old woman, she moved very fast. She hobbled around Marian, then all of a sudden, she stood still, watching Marian intently. After a minute or two, she tottered over to a shelf and reached for a pot of some form of liquid. Alan and Robin stood close to the door, out of Grishelda's way. She went over to Marian and placed the liquid by her nose.

Alan watched, relief washing over him, as Marian awoke and for a moment, she seemed herself. Until she doubled over and paled; his heart sunk.

"Uncle, no! Get away!" He had often heard her call out in her dreams, waking him in the manor, but this was different. He longed to comfort Marian, but he knew he should not.

He kept back to make sure he did not hinder Grishelda's help, but she was already working too slowly.

"Please do something. Can you not see? She is suffering!" he blurted out without a thought.

Grishelda's head turned sharply to Alan and he quieted instantly. That look really *could* kill. Grishelda snapped back to the task at hand and went over to another shelf. She smelled various liquids until she brought one over to Alan and Robin, mumbling something to herself that Alan could not hear.

"This is the one. I have only had a couple of cases before – stronger doses. I did not get a chance to treat them." Alan gulped, trying to release the lump in his throat. The others had died. "Perhaps she has a chance. She is trying to fight it. She is strong, but she does not have long. I think I know a cure. We must use another poison as an antidote. It should work." Should, perhaps. That did not sound promising.

"Worth a try," Robin agreed quietly.

"Ah well, I do not have it in my possession. The plant is grown a few miles north of here. It is deadly and only I know where it is. I will have to leave her and go myself. You must dampen her forehead to fight off the fever and keep talking to her. Try to keep her awake. Use my smelling oils on that shelf over there," she pointed to the shelf to the left of the door. "I will be back soon. Robert, I need to borrow some of your men. I do not want to run into any unforgiving folk, do I?" Robert? Was that Robin's real name? There was too much for Alan to get his head around.

Robin opened the door, waiting for Grishelda to follow. Alan watched helplessly as she collected supplies for the journey, she then followed Robin out. He was left alone with Marian. What had the woman said? Wet her forehead. He looked around, unsure what was safe and unsafe. He found a bowl of water that looked clean enough and a material of some sort that might work. He pulled out a chair from under the table Marian lay on. It was covered in dust, but he did not bother to clear it. He placed the bowl on the floor beside him and wet the cloth, then placed it on her forehead. He looked down at Marian; she was unconscious again. He had to keep her awake. He rushed over to the shelf to the left of the door, forgetting the bowl of water on the floor and tripped over it. Water spilled everywhere but he managed to salvage a little of it, placing the bowl further from him. It was very unlike him to be so clumsy. He grabbed a liquid from the shelf, opened the lid and put it to Marian's nose like Grishelda had done. This time, Marian woke slower, slurring her speech. She was getting worse.

"Marian. You have to stay awake. You hear me?"

"Just kill me," she breathed. "I deserve it."

"You're delusional. It is the poison." Then, as a note to himself, added "I will kill Gisbourne."

She winced. "No, you do not understand. He was under orders."

"He does what he likes. He cares nothing for orders."

Marian shook her head slightly. "New Sheriff... back..." She tried to take a deep breath, gulping in the air.

"Marian, do not make yourself worse. It can wait."

"No!" she tried to shout, but it sounded more like she was being strangled.

"Alright, take it slowly. The new Sheriff, you know him?" Marian nodded, unable to do much else. Alan noticed her starting to slip into unconsciousness again. He stood, shaking her arms. "You have to stay awake."

"Let me sleep," she slurred.

"No, Marian. Remember you need to tell me something. Focus on that. The Sheriff is someone you used to know? And… he controls Gisbourne?"

"Yes… He came to kill me."

"Is he from your past?" He meant to say perhaps the one who hurt her, but he could not bring himself to say it.

Marian nodded, her eyes watering from the pain. "Make it stop. I killed them. I am guilty!"

At that moment, Robin stormed in with such urgency that the door flew into the wall and shook the hut, the containers rattling on the shelves. Alan looked up at him, stunned.

"You are making her worse!" Robin shouted. He paused, and Alan could see the ongoing battle between his emotions. "What is she talking about?"

"You would not understand. It is too much to explain," Alan said bitterly. He had not meant for it to come out like that, but Robin was not making the situation any easier.

"Robin, what happened?" Marian asked groggily. Alan stepped back, letting Robin speak to her.

"What do you mean?" he asked, his voice calmer.

"You left me. You were not there. I was late… He found me… would not let me leave…" She was trying to scratch her back.

"Here, let me help."

"NO!"

Alan knew what she was doing. He had seen the scars on her back. He interpreted that when Robin and Marian used to know each other, she was going to run off with him, but she never turned up. Then it clicked. Her uncle, she had told him he was cruel. And all those nightmares; crying out in her sleep. That man had given her those scars, and he had come back for her, to finish the job. Robin started towards Marian's back to try and help.

"Robin, stay back. She does not want you to see…" Before he could finish and just before Robin was about to see her back, Marian screamed in agony. This was it; she was going to die. Alan replaced the damp cloth on her forehead, trying to do anything to help. Marian was getting weaker. Robin stood by the door again and Alan looked at him, silently asking him to help her, but he just stood there uselessly. Marian's body stopped moving. He looked at her, dread creeping in, but she was not dead yet. She was breathing in short, fast pants, and she was looking at him.

Marian searched for something to focus on, anything to ease the pain, a coping mechanism she had taught herself to calm the pain of her scars. She found solace in Alan's eyes, his familiar face. She was safe here: safe to die and safe from her uncle. This was the end. She could feel darkness blocking the corners of her vision, but she kept her eyes on Alan. She could no longer see Robin. Did he leave? Did she mean that little to him? Alan's face warped into her uncle. She could not tell the difference between reality and her fevered visions. She closed her eyes blocking everything out and the world went silent.

Chapter 18

Tuck waited and waited outside Grishelda's home. He wanted to help, but his talents lay elsewhere. Instead he spent the night sat outside, leaning against the hut. When Marian had first arrived in Nottingham, she had visited him on many occasions, and they had walked to church together. They both shared a love for the architecture and beauty of a church. She had always talked freely with him of God and what amazed him was that she still came to church even though she had never believed. It had made him question whether Christianity was indeed a religion or whether it was just the rules of being a good person. He still did not know to this day. He had no idea what triggered him to leave the church, whether it be God or fate, as Marian had put it to him. They seemed like the same thing, but all he could do to help in this situation was pray. He did not know if his prayers would be heard, but even if there was a God, he would probably not answer his prayers after the sins he had committed. He prayed half-heartedly, afraid of himself more than the wrath of God, but he had to try at least. He decided that whether she live or die, he would return to Nottingham. Tuck felt somewhere deep inside that his purpose was in Nottingham, and he could not leave the people to suffer under the new Sheriff's rule. But first, he had to wait until Marian's fate was decided.

He had fallen asleep from exhaustion during the night and awoke to Grishelda returning. Tuck could wait no longer, and, truth be told, he was cold. After a few minutes, he opened the door just enough to look inside.

"Is she going to be alright?" Alan asked. Tuck looked to Grishelda, wanting to know the truth as much as Alan. He could tell by the uncertainty on the woman's face that it was a risk. Nobody knew what side effects Marian could get from it, or even whether it would help in any way.

"I know as much as you. It has definitely done something. She is not dead, and that is a good sign." Why did she have to point out the obvious?

Tuck did not notice Robin in the room until suddenly the door was pulled fully open from inside, revealing Tuck to everyone inside. Robin looked at him with tired eyes, and Tuck stepped aside for him. Robin was acting very strange. He would not have been surprised if Robin had pushed him out of the way, but he had simply stood there, as though he had no fight left in him. Tuck wandered back outside, embarrassed by his obvious intrusion, and hoped Marian would pull through. *Some things are worse than death.*

He left without a word to anyone, though no one would miss him. Tuck was good at navigating his way around, he had learnt it as a young boy in the church. Follow the stars and God will see you home.

#

Marian felt peaceful in her slumber. Finally, the pain had stopped. She did not know if she was dead. Perhaps this was what it felt like; light as a feather, all the burdens of life released. There were voices somewhere far away, but she did not listen. She was happy, resolute. Here there were no threats, no enemies. She closed her eyes, took a deep breath, and opened her eyes to a burning light. For a moment, she believed she had ended up in hell. And it was hell. *I am alive.*

Faces looked down at her and she sat up. Her whole body throbbed in protest.

"Easy. There you go." Alan was there. She did not know what she had said in her fevered mind. She prayed he did not know the whole truth. She let Alan lower her carefully back to a comfortable position. How comfortable could a table be though? Not very, she laughed inwardly. Marian's eyes stung with exhaustion, but she knew this time her nightmares would return. They always did. Why could they not just let her die? It would be a release. Perhaps that would be her torment, never free of the pain of her past. She truly believed everyone would be a lot safer without her.

"Eat." Suddenly a woman was pushing Alan aside, holding out a bowl of liquid Marian did not like the look of.

"Who are you?"

"Me, well I just saved your life. You go on though. Do not worry yourself about me," she said bitterly. Marian obeyed, and let the woman feed her. After she was finished, the woman stormed off, and under her breath said "I am going to bed. If you need me, find someone else," then slammed the door behind her.

"Moody," Alan said, mimicking the woman's voice. Marian laughed, and stopped abruptly when her muscles tensed painfully. "Sorry. Oh, that was Grishelda. Robin knows her somehow. What a character, ay?" Marian nodded. She was not sure what to say. "What you said, I still cannot piece everything together," he said, more seriously.

"I do not really remember much after you found me."

"Oh. Well…you said the new Sheriff is your uncle?"

All of the events of the previous day came flooding back and Marian could not stop the tears from flowing down her cheeks.

"Did I say something wrong? Did I get it wrong?"

"Everything is a mess. There is no way to fix it." She did not have a filter anymore. The walls she had spent years putting up to protect herself had come crashing down, and she was more vulnerable than she had ever been in her life.

"Please tell me. Tell me everything. It will help you, you know. I promise I will not tell anyone, even Robin."

"I know, I trust you. There is just too much that has happened, that cannot be fixed." She took a deep breath. She needed to tell him. He had to know what a horrid person she was, that she was as corrupt as her uncle.

"My uncle brought me up when my mother died and my father could not cope with me. He was a wealthy man, in a big manor. But he wanted to turn me into something I could not become. He hated me. He hated that I could not be that person. He…" She did not know how to explain, without it sounding cruel. "…used violence." She paused, struggling to actually talk about it, after so many years of lying to herself as well as everyone else. Before, she could almost believe it never actually happened, that her life started when she came to Nottingham, but now it would all be true. It would be real.

"Take your time Marian. There is no rush." Her hands were shaking from the pressure of the situation, even though she knew there was no pressure on her telling the truth, but it was more a fight against instinct to get the truth out.

"The maids were kind to me. Every day they would sneak me out the servants' entrance, just for an hour. I always took the same route through the forest; it was calming to be outside in the fresh air, away from the darkness and the danger of the manor. One day, it was the anniversary of my mother's death and I was not thinking straight. I got lost on my walk and bumped into a young boy, Robin." She did not want to tell him about Robin. It was private and for some reason she wanted it to stay that way. "He told me I could join his outlaws and run away with them. I promised to meet him the next morning when the outlaws were going to move somewhere different. I never got there. When I went to leave, my uncle was waiting for me, expecting me." She could not bring herself to say aloud what happened next. Even thinking about it brought back the memories. She clutched the table, like a weight had fallen upon her.

"Marian, are you alright?" Alan looked worried. She took another deep breath.

"I almost died. The servants saved me and…" The memory of their faces came to Marian's mind. *I killed them. They saved my life and I killed them.*

"Marian, stop! You are hurting yourself."

Marian looked down, dazed. Her hands gripped onto the table with such force that some of the wood had splintered, cutting her hands. She looked at them, feeling empty. She let Alan clean the wounds and wrap bandages around them. She could not face looking at him directly. Alan sat back, letting her take her time. She sensed he did not mind whether she spoke or not, but it was a comfort that he stayed.

Finally, Marian forced herself to look Alan in the eyes, and it slipped out. "I killed them."

"What are you talking about? Marian, you did not kill anyone. You kept saying this in your fever. Should I wake Grishelda?"

"Those ruins were my uncle's manor. All the servants died because of me." She had not meant to say it, and there was nothing else to say. She needed to get away. She needed to clear her head. Marian sat up slowly.

"What are you doing?"

"I need some air."

"You need rest."

Marian looked at him quizzically. "I need to rest? Nobody tells me what to do! I should be dead. I deserve it. Those servants, my friends died. They *died* because of me."

"Listen to me; it is not your fault."

She ignored him, looking down at herself. She still wore her own dress, smelling from the events of yesterday. She carefully stood, not even caring to put any shoes on. She did not care about the pain in her body. In fact, it was a reminder that she was alive. She could hear Alan's footsteps behind, following, but he did not try to stop her.

"Where are you going?" Robin called in the distance.

"For a walk," Alan replied. She had to get away.

Marian did not mean to go anywhere in particular, she just let her legs carry her. She could breathe again, feeling the fresh air fill her lungs. The smell of summer, warm and blossoming, filled her senses. It was like a dream, it reminded her of limbo, floating on a cloud. A weight had lifted. Then she looked around.

"No," she whispered in disbelief. Marian stood in the clearing where she had first met Robin. Cold realisation hit her like a slap to the face. *If I had not met Robin, I would have stayed with uncle. I might have lived, I might have died. But they would have been safe.*

"Marian?" She whirled, recognising the voice.

"Robin? I am here, like I promised. Where are the others?"

"What others? What are you talking about Marian?"

"I managed to get away. I am joining you all, remember? Yesterday, you told me I could join you and we could have adventures together."

"Marian, that was years ago. We have not seen each other for a long time. I waited for you, but you did not show up. I had to leave without you."

"But I…" Marian's world came crashing down.

"Marian, it is alright. You will be alright. It is just the effects of the poison wearing off. I am going to take you back."

She panicked. "Back home? You cannot take me there! He will kill me for sure!"

"Marian?" Someone else was there. She turned, following the direction of the voice. "Alan, remember? You trust me. You were poisoned by your uncle and we saved you. We will not take you home. We will take you to a safe place." Marian fell to her knees. Her past would never stop haunting her.

Over the next few days, Alan kept close watch over Marian. She was grateful for him, but she did not deserve such a kind gesture. Every day she felt a little more like herself, but she could not stop the flashbacks. She did not tell Alan anything else; she was too fearful that it might set her off again. But the more she felt like herself, the more lost she became. She had no home to go to and the truths her uncle had told her haunted her daily life, not just the nightmares. She did not know who she was anymore.

#

"Robin, thank you for meeting me." Alan walked towards his leader. Robin had left when Marian's condition started to improve. He had taken the majority of his men but left just a few to protect Grishelda's home while Marian recovered. Yesterday Alan had sent a messenger to request to meet with Robin.

"What do you need to talk about?" Robin got straight to the point.

"It is about Marian…"

"Has something happened to her?" Robin interrupted before he could finish.

"No. She has been through a lot. She does not have a home."

"She does, in Nottingham. You said so yourself."

"She cannot go back. She is lost and needs something to take her mind off things. Robin surely after everything, you could give her some help."

"Why can she not return to Nottingham? It is her home after all. At least she has one. I have helped her enough. I am busy, do not waste my time." Alan could not believe Robin's attitude towards Marian. He could tell Robin was trying to hide his emotions again, but it was not working. His wall had come down and there was nothing that could return Robin to how he used to be no matter how hard he tried. Alan hoped it was for the better, at least he was showing some emotion, even if it was impatience.

Alan had promised Marian to never tell anyone what she had told him. He kept his word. "Well the fact that she was poisoned might have something to do with it. Gisbourne is a powerful man. She cannot return. She will not be safe."

"You have a point. What do you suggest? Set up a new life for her? That is not something I can really help with, is it? If I could set up a new life for people, do you think we would all be having to live in the forest, fighting every day to survive?"

"That is what the people are already doing! Do you think, that because they have a home to live in, their lives are secure and happy? Because they are not. They are threatened in different ways than us, from powerful people who are greedy for money. At least we have freedom; the people are trapped."

"What do you suggest then? The only life I can offer, is to become an outlaw, and that is outrageous."

"Why? If a man can become an outlaw, why not a woman? I am sure there are plenty of women who break the law and survive in the forest. Grishelda for instance?"

"Grishelda barely counts. She is a harsh, tough woman who has enough potions and poisons to wipe out an entire town! Marian is a Lady."

"I heard you were once a lord when you were young. How times have changed. You toughened up, you became an outlaw. What makes her so different?"

"My lands were taken away when I was five years old. All I have known is life as an outlaw."

"Your father, then. Connor had been a very powerful lord before he made a mistake, and he adapted well. I think having an entire gang practically worship him proved his success."

"For one, his affair was much more than a mistake. And I inherited his gang, just like he had wanted me to. I had no choice in the matter, even though at the end he despised me."

"For someone who has been an outlaw for so long, you talk like a pompous noble. You always have a choice, Robin. You could have walked away from all this, tried to start a new life for yourself, but you stayed."

"Why are you turning this on me? I am your leader, you should not talk to me like this."

"Really, Robin? I am only telling you the truth. Whether you want to hear it or not, you are no better than Marian. In fact, Marian is probably better than all of us. Everything that has happened to her was not brought on by her own actions. We make mistakes and we deal with the consequences. She has done no wrong, and yet has been punished all her life."

He had said too much, more than Marian would have wanted Robin to know.

"You are right. Marian is a good person, and I am not. She is a far greater person than I will ever be. So just accept that and leave me alone."

"I did not mean it like that. You are changing Robin, for the better, I think. You are just as lost as Marian, and she needs us right now."

"She should marry some rich fellow who can protect her."

"You cannot think of women in such low regard. Marian can take care of herself. She is skilled."

"What, in cooking? Cleaning? We could do with that in camp, but I do not think she would like that much."

Alan was tired of Robin's bitterness. "Just… give her a trial. You cannot say no to that. She is good with a bow and arrow. You saw that wound on Arthur's arm; she did that. Please give her a chance, I think she needs this. And if she does not fit in, if it does not work, then we will go elsewhere."

"Alright. You have yourself a deal. Bring her to camp tomorrow."

It had been almost two weeks since Beatrice and Alice had last seen Marian, leaving for the castle after Walter died. Emma had come over the next day and explained that Alan had been imprisoned but Tuck had helped him escape. Marian was in danger but Alan and Tuck were going to save her with the help of some outlaws.

Beatrice was not convinced that outlaws would help Marian. They were nasty people, although the only outlaws she had ever met were the ones who had broken into their home. She had grown increasingly anxious when she had not heard anything, not even a whisper since. Beatrice had kept herself occupied by watching and supporting Alice's training. She herself had visited the castle to try and find out where Marian was several days ago, only to be turned away by the guards at the front gate. She even attempted to bribe them, but to no avail.

Finally, she had gone to Tuck, whom she knew Marian visited often. He had been drunker than she had ever seen a man act before. She found him sat in the tavern. Beatrice had always stayed far away from him before, unwilling to see the devil who had renounced God. She always worried that she would receive God's wrath for being connected to someone who went against every belief in the church. She had to push her worries aside as she sat next to him. *God forgive me.*

"Do you know anything of Marian?"

"Why do you want to know?" He slurred his words as he spoke.

"I am one of Marian's maids. I have known her as long as you have, and I am so worried. Please tell me she is safe." It was not like her to be so mannered, but she was desperate to find out if Marian was alright.

"You do not like me."

"You are a heathen. You reject God and God in turn rejects you. I should not be associated with such a devil, but I am desperate."

Tuck gave a full bellied laugh, and then stopped abruptly, so much so that everyone in the tavern turned to face him. Everyone was used to Tuck being a quiet man, drunk or not, but this was very strange behaviour. He threw his half empty drink across the room and it struck the wall and chimed as it fell to the floor. Beatrice watched in shock as he stood and sobered straight away. He stormed out and she followed behind.

Beatrice followed Tuck around back streets and finally stopped on the outskirts of Nottingham, close to Marian's home. He turned to face Beatrice.

"Marian was poisoned by the Sheriff and Gisbourne. She was recovering when I last saw her, but do not expect her to come back too soon. She will not be safe here, so for now it is best everyone believes she is gone."

"For now? You mean she will return?"

"I know nothing for certain, but something big is starting. Can you feel it?"

And with that, he turned and left. She was left stunned by his words, but Marian was safe and that was all that mattered. Perhaps Tuck was not as Godless as she had thought. He saw things that only a believer would be able to see.

When she returned, Alice was teaching herself to throw blades.

"Take it easy, Alice. I do not want you hurting yourself, or me for that matter."

"I am always careful, see?" Beatrice watched as Alice carefully aimed the blade and threw it. It landed dead centre, embedded in the tree.

"You really are a miniature Marian. I should start a regiment of female soldiers," she joked.

"You are cheery today, Beatrice. You have news!" Alice looked at her with excited eyes, reminding Beatrice that Alice was still only a child in her eyes.

"Yes, she is safe and alive. She cannot return home yet, as there are threats in Nottingham. Those in power want her gone, so we need to make them believe she is dead." A deep smile warmed Alice's face from the marks of anxiety that had creased her forehead for weeks. Alice was a beauteous young lady and every day she was growing to become more and more like Marian. Beatrice's family would be whole again soon. But in the back of her mind, Tuck's words tormented her. Something big was starting. And Beatrice *could* feel it.

Chapter 19

Marian was nervous about meeting Robin's gang. From the way Alan had explained it to her, the outlaws would react badly to a noble woman becoming one of them. She needed to prove herself, somehow. Thinking about it, Marian did not know what outlaws actually spent their time doing, other than robbing anyone who passed through the forest. In a way, it excited her. She had a new purpose, something to keep her occupied, while she tried to figure her life out. She followed Alan into camp.

Looking around, Marian was surprised that the camp was so small and bland looking. She had expected there to be stolen goods everywhere, decorating the camp like a home, but this was just another part of the forest. It was a small clearing, at the top of a hill. Strategically placed so they would be able to see enemies approaching. Marian joked inwardly that they did have brains after all. There were a couple of fur coats as well as sheets and other warm blankets set out where the outlaws slept. A few logs lay around the centre of camp, where a small fire burned. She should have expected the lack of homeliness; outlaws never stayed in the same place for too long, it meant they could make a quick getaway. She already missed her home with her large warm bed and layer upon layer of covers. This was going to be a big change compared to what she was used to.

Whatever introduction she expected to receive, this was not the way Marian imagined it at all. The moment she walked into camp, everyone stopped what they were doing and glared at her, unimpressed with what they saw. There were only three of them, as well as Alan, though Marian remembered there being a lot more. Robin was not around either; her heart contracted at the thought. He must have taken some of his outlaws on an errand...a job? She did not know their coded language and was an outsider, a misfit to them. It reminded her of when she first moved to Nottingham, although there she could at least hide herself away.

Here, she was out in the open and there was nowhere to hide.

One of the men, who had been sat on a log around the fire, stood. He was a giant, tall and broad. He looked as though he was strong enough to kill a man with his bare hands. He was a fair distance from her, but she took a step back instinctively.

"This is no place for a girl," he bellowed.

"Robin said to give her a chance." The man lying on a fur coat strode over to the giant, smirking. The giant sat back down and the man turned towards Marian. "I think we should see what she is made of," he said, studying her.

"Is that what you suggest?" Alan asked, interrupting before the men could say anything else. They all agreed in unison. They seemed to know each other very well. Another quiet man lay a little further from the rest of them, but he still joined in agreement. "Alright. But first introduce yourselves to her. It is a lot to take in."

"Fine, have it your way," the man standing next to the giant said childishly. He turned to Marian. "Well, my name is Will Scarlett. Pleasure, my Lady," he curtseyed, patronising her. He was the joker of the gang, she had no time for clowns.

"John, Little John," said the giant. *A fitting name*, Marian thought.

"Little you are not, John," Will butted in again. Marian was already growing tiresome of him, but Little John rolled his eyes and she knew she was not the only one. She at least had that in common with Little John. She relaxed a little.

"And that over there is the tortured soul. Introduce yourself, we have a guest!" Will shouted to the man who sat away from the rest. There was no need to be so rude to him. The man turned around, noticing everyone staring at him, and walked over. He was thin and small, and looked more like a boy than a man, with no facial hair unlike the rest of them, and little confidence. As he walked, he looked at the ground the whole way.

"Tobias, nice to meet you," he mumbled, then sat on another log by the fire, turned away from the others.

"Is that all of you?" Marian wondered. They all laughed suddenly. Had she made a joke? She blushed, embarrassed.

"Of course not! We are the best of the bunch, although not quite sure what little Tobias is doing here. Robin obviously wanted you to meet us lovely chaps before meeting the animals." Will was getting on Marian's nerves already but

114

she bit her tongue, the pain easing some of her tension. "Alright. You are the serious kind. I get it. You are all so serious. It is so dull."

"Now you understand how we feel about you," Little John replied.

"You actually made a joke?"

"That was not a joke."

Alan stopped the argument from getting out of control. "Right, shall we get down to business? You want Marian to prove herself. Marian, are you up for that?"

"Of course, what do you want me to do?" Marian was eager to actually get around to doing something.

"Cook!" Will demanded. "A proper meal! I miss a good meal. The others are awful at cooking. It is barely edible."

"You think I know how to cook? Because I am a woman?" Will nodded excitedly. He was acting like a silly little child. She was getting frustrated. "Sorry to disappoint but I do not cook."

"Ooh rich lady. Do you have servants to cook for you?"

"That is enough, Will. You do not know anything about Marian. She does not cook. Give her a real test," Alan amended.

"How about clean our clothes or make our beds or..." Marian stopped listening. She had an idea that would shock Will out of his wits. Alan was turned away from Marian. She snuck up on him, taking his dagger and flung it. Will yelped, seeing the dagger flying towards him and it struck home.

Marian laughed; she could not help herself. His face was a pale picture of shock and horror. He looked down slowly and between his legs the dagger was stuck deep into the log that he had sat down on. For once he was silent, everyone was silent. Even Little John looked surprised.

"I think you killed his humour. Well done. We have been trying to do that for years," Alan laughed. At that, Little John started laughing too, and even Tobias giggled.

This is not actually that bad, Marian thought to herself. *I could get used to this*.

A few hours passed and Marian enjoyed the outlaws' company. She had not yet seen Robin, nor any of the other outlaws. Alan explained to her that Robin often travelled to different places, after the best merchandise to steal. Sometimes rumours would spread about a big steal. The messengers on lookout duty would hear close to towns and villages that a large load would be travelling through the forest and they would report back to Robin. Alan suggested it must be a very big steal for them to be away so long. Marian was interested to see how they went about their thieving. She did not know what it entailed, whether they had a plan in place or just went along with it. She wanted to experience real outlaw life, but at the moment, all they seemed to do was sit around, waiting for Robin.

"Can you not go off on your own and do what you want?"

"We wait. Robin always returns and there is always another steal," Will replied. Even he sounded bored, his humour fading.

"But you just sit around doing nothing. Is that not dull to you?" Marian could not believe it. She thought their lives would be more exciting and adventurous than this.

"Robin is our leader. What he says goes," Little John replied.

"What if one day, he never returned? Would you just wait until you died here, sitting on this very log?" That got their attention. They all looked at each other suspiciously. To Marian it looked like they had never actually thought about it that way before.

"He always comes back," was all Tobias said.

"How do you make the time pass?"

"We hunt, we eat. We collect supplies for winter," Will cited, as though it were their bible, their religion.

"How exactly do you survive winter? There are enough deaths in the cities alone, where there are fires and beds and shelter."

Alan jumped into the conversation, trying to explain. "We find shelter, usually in a cave somewhere. We have several that we travel between each year. That is why we collect supplies through the warmer months, so we can try our best to survive the winter. Not many travel into the forests in winter so there are no fresh pickings and we simply wait out the cold, until it starts to warm."

"All you seem to do is wait," Marian whined impatiently. "Well I for one need something to do. Any ideas?"

"Cook?" Will queried, making Marian's blood boil.

"Here," Alan announced. "I will show you how to craft a bow and arrow. Remember, my family made a living out of making weapons. Then you can get back to your training." He gave her something to focus on.

Marian's heart sunk. She was reminded that she had started training with Alice. She had neglected Alice and Beatrice. They must have no idea what had happened to her.

"I forgot about Beatrice and Alice. They must be so worried."

"Emma helped Tuck and I escape from the gaol and promised to tell Beatrice we were going to save you. I am sure they are fine Marian. They know you can take care of yourself. They will look after your home for you."

"That is not my home," Marian said instinctively. She did not have a home. And Nottingham could never be a home to her again, her uncle had made sure of that. He must have suspected her dead by now.

Marian watched Alan make the bow. It took time and skill, she realised. She watched the entirety of it, from collecting the yew wood, to sanding down the shape and attaching the string. It was oddly comforting but it made her miss her manor in Nottingham.

"Here," Alan gave her the bow. She stretched it, examining every part. It really was a beautiful bow; far more intricate than the basic one she had trained with. "I will carve some arrows for you to practice with."

"Thank you," and she really meant it.

Marian looked down at herself. Her dress was grimy and smelling and she needed a bath. "What do you do around here to get clean?" she wondered.

"We wait until it rains," Will butted in, surprising her, as he had been sleeping a moment before. She could not tell if he was serious or not, so looked to Alan for confirmation.

"That or we find a source of water to bathe in. There is nothing near here, so rain might be the best option right now," Alan said matter-of-fact.

"Any clue when it might rain?"

"Welcome to the disgusting life of an outlaw. We do not have luxuries like baths here, Lady," Will said sarcastically.

Marian ignored him. She desperately needed to change too. "And what do you do for clothes?"

"We steal," Little John replied. He was so straightforward; she decided that she liked him.

"In that chest over there, there might be some clothes that fit you," Alan said helpfully. He pointed to near a stack of warm blankets, where Marian noticed an old, wooden chest. She wondered over and opened it.

A few trousers and shirts; nothing for a woman, but she was not a woman right now. She was an outlaw. She had to think like an outlaw. Marian had always longed for the comfort of men's clothes; to be able to wear practical trousers. She pulled out the smallest things she could find. Marian searched for a spot to dress without them seeing her. It was not a normal sort of embarrassment, dressing in front of men, but it was her scars. She could not bear for anyone else to judge her by her past. She believed that was why Alan had become so protective over her.

"What is the matter? Shy to change around men?" Will remarked. "I cannot promise I will not look. I have not seen a woman's body in quite some time." He winked at her.

"She should not have to dress in front of you, especially after that comment." Alan said, looking around. Marian watched as he went through the pile of blankets next to the chest of clothes. He picked long, dirty sheets out of the pile and walked towards a cluster of trees. He tied the materials to the tree in a square, like a wall, covering every side.

"Here you are. Your own bit of privacy," Alan said, loud enough for the others to hear. He then quieted his voice to a whisper. "Sorry, it is the best I can do," he added regretfully.

"It is perfect, thank you." Marian genuinely felt touched by his gesture.

She got changed quickly, simply because she did not completely trust these men yet. They were outlaws after all, and they were not used to the company of a woman. She felt stronger somehow, dressed like a man. She could move a lot easier than in a dress. The clothes were dull greens and browns, similar to the other outlaws. That must be how they hide so well in the forest, blending in with their surroundings. They were craftier than Marian had given them credit for.

When Marian appeared from her little den, Alan was waiting with some practical shoes. He handed them to her, and she took them gratefully, putting them on. They were a little big for her, but she did not complain.

As if on cue, several outlaws appeared from nowhere and lastly Robin stepped into camp. He looked tired, with shadows under his eyes, she could tell even from a distance. None of the outlaws looked happy. Marian felt like she was interrupting something so decided to stay where she was and observe from a distance.

Little John, Will and Tobias stood, greeting their fellow outlaws. Most of the men she had never seen before ignored them and went about various distractions. Nobody noticed her and she did not mind. She hated being the centre of attention. Something felt wrong though, darkness had fallen, and it was too silent for so many men.

"What happened?" Little John asked gravely, sensing the same bad feeling Marian felt.

"I am glad I did not take my best men. We lost a few. It was a trap, set by Gisbourne no doubt. He seems more dangerous than ever. He had many guards with him. He must have a lot of power to be able to command that many."

Marian spoke without thinking. "I knew it. He is the Sheriff of Nottingham's right-hand man. He has all the power he would ever need. And now that he thinks I am dead, he is putting his energies back into hunting down outlaws. You should not play along with his game. It is a dangerous one." Marian then realised her place and apologised quietly, stepping back. Robin looked at her, surprised. Why was everyone always surprised by her? She did not understand it.

"It was no game to us, Marian. Could you have done any better?"

"I…" She did not know how to respond to such a statement.

"She does have a point. We need to be careful with Gisbourne. He will stop at nothing to get what he wants. I have seen it myself." Alan shared a look with Marian. She knew he was thinking of when Gisbourne had invaded her home and tried to force her to marry him, his true self revealing to be a predator.

At that, Marian could feel Robin studying her, analysing her.

"I believe you, I have seen it myself. We should move to smaller targets for now, just to be safe. Tomorrow, we will find a steal and Marian, you can join us. See what it is really like to be an outlaw."

Chapter 20

Marian did not sleep well that night. It was not just in anticipation for her first ever steal, but she had not realised before how cold it got at night. She had never slept under the stars, and although it was strangely comforting to watch the night sky, it was also very dangerous and cold. Even in the heat of the summer, at night the temperature plummeted. She had grabbed only one blanket when the outlaws went to sleep, having copied the other men. However, they were used to sleeping outside and this was probably pretty warm to them compared to winter. They also kept their weapons close to them, just in case anyone was to attack, or any animals came too close. After a while, she had quietly grabbed a couple of extra blankets and slept near the remains of the fire; only then was she warm enough.

Marian finally managed to sleep, but only for an hour or two. She awoke just before sunrise. Today she would see what being an outlaw was all about, not just sitting around waiting for something to happen. This was just what she had wanted. It was a chance to really prove herself. And now, thanks to Alan, she had a brand-new bow ready just in case she might encounter any resistance.

Marian felt free and alive, living in the wilderness. As the sky began to brighten, Marian quietly moved away from the outlaws and watched the sunrise, lighting up the darkness of the forest. It was a glorious sight often overseen, but it truly was beautiful. She breathed in clean air, catching the scent of wild flowers in the soft breeze. This was an adventure, but it was not yet her home. Perhaps one day it could be. And at that she felt a pang of longing for Nottingham, for Walter. She wished she had gotten a chance to properly say goodbye to him, but it would have been impossible. There had not even been a funeral procession to attend, which filled her with rage. Her uncle had even taken that away from her.

Even though he had not managed to kill her yet, she had lost almost everything else to him, and this was worse in a way. He probably would not even be that angry that she was still alive, knowing she was suffering more in life than she would in death, and he would revel in it.

She had an upper hand on the Sheriff right now, though. He believed she was dead, and she wanted it to stay that way. Marian was safe knowing he was not searching for her anymore. She promised herself she would go back one day, to bid a final farewell to Walter. She owed him that much at least.

Slowly the men awoke, and she watched them prepare for the task ahead. Marian did not know what it would entail, and nobody seemed to want to explain it to her either. She guessed she would watch this from the side lines, to get a feel for what they did. She waited, holding her bow, for someone to tell her what to do.

#

Alan did not really want to be an outlaw again, he had thought the life of thievery had been behind him, but he was doing this for Marian, he reminded himself. It was not pleasant work, but she had wanted to become an outlaw and he could not turn her down. He hoped she would not be upset or angry at him for the person he used to be. He wondered if it would be different now that he had tasted a normal life once more. Perhaps he had lost his taste for this kind of life, always on the run, but it came all too naturally to him. He managed to find Robin barking orders to some of the messengers.

Alan could tell Robin was nervous about the lack of supplies they had obtained to get them through the next winter. There were only a few months left until they would need to rely completely on the supplies. Robin was becoming more authoritative than he had ever been before and Alan sensed everyone was on edge because of it. He waited until Robin had let one group on their way.

"Robin. What is your plan for Marian today?"

"Oh." It was clear to Alan there were other things on his mind. "You take care of her, keep her close to you and do not let her get involved. She would probably ruin everything. I cannot lose another steal, or any more lives right now." Robin turned and left at that, his mind busy with the burdens of being a leader.

That did not give Alan much confidence. If Robin was worried, then they should all be worried. It meant bad news for everyone.

#

Marian was starting to think everyone had forgotten her, until finally Alan approached her, holding a makeshift crate for Marian's arrows to go in.

"Now, Marian. I have been instructed that you need to stay close to me at all times. For each steal, there are always a few of us on watch, patrolling the area to make sure we are not ambushed nor have any unwanted visitors. That will be our job today. But we will stay close to the steal so you can see what happens. Beware though, it can get quite messy." Marian turned to him to ask what he meant by that, but he was already walking away. She followed close behind.

Even though all the outlaws were preparing themselves, it seemed they were going in different directions, perhaps to different tasks set by Robin. Marian did not yet understand how their system worked, although they seemed very organised, compared to the chaos she had expected. As small groups left in opposite directions, she noticed, with relief, Robin at the front of her group. Now Marian would get to see the real Robin. Her heart fluttered, but she forced the feeling down. He did not want her here, why was she hoping otherwise?

Marian looked around to see whether anyone she recognised was going with them. Out of the outlaws she had personally met, only Tobias, Alan and Robin were in her group. It was a very small team, Marian had thought there would be at least ten to twenty, but there were only two others who Marian had not seen before. The total, including Marian was a mere six. She felt like she was part of an army, different sections sent off to defend from different angles. And off to battle they went.

It felt strange not to march or have any order. They walked in a small huddle, very casually, as if nothing could endanger them, although Marian knew that was far from the truth. The forest, for all its beauty, was also a place of danger. Wild animals roamed free and crazed men were known to hide out, waiting for their next victim. At least, that was what she understood from the stories Walter used to tell her. And, she realised, she would never hear his voice again.

Marian forced herself to forget about Walter for now. She was meant to be distracting herself from her mind, it was not working thus far.

Nobody talked the whole way. All she could hear were their footsteps thumping the ground in no particular rhythm, until finally they all came to a standstill, gathering around Robin.

"With any luck, the cart should be travelling through here in a few minutes. Lucas, Pit and Tobias…" he paused, listening. Marian heard a faint bird whistle, but it was too clear to actually be a bird. It must be a signal to Robin about something. "I will be right back."

"Does he often do that?" Marian asked quietly.

Alan shrugged. "He only tells us what we need to know. It takes the pressure off us. He makes all the decisions."

"Does it never bother you that he may be making the wrong decisions, if you have no clue what he knows? He could be sending you to your deaths." She did not understand their undying loyalty to Robin. Surely a fair leader would share information and not be so secretive.

All Alan replied was: "Everyone here has secrets."

Robin returned hastily, his expression unreadable. "I have to sort something out. You all know what you are doing." He did not even acknowledge Marian, but Alan did not question it. She did not know what she was doing. "I will meet you back at camp later." At that, Robin was gone.

Marian looked quizzically at everyone. Who was going to take charge? Nobody was stepping up. "Do any of you actually know what you are doing?"

"Of course, I just did not expect him to go off like that. Usually we have some direction. Something serious must be happening for him to leave so suddenly," Alan observed. Everyone was looking at him. "Oh, you want me to take charge? I am a little out of practice. But I guess I have been doing this the longest. Tobias, stay with Marian. You have only stood watch before, so you know what you are doing with that. Lucas and Pit, you are well practiced, you lead the steal with me. I guess we are on our own. Everyone take your places. By what Robin said, the cart should be here soon. Any problems give the signal."

Marian followed Tobias, who had not so much as looked at Marian. Did he remember he was meant to be showing her the ropes? She had looked forward to watching Robin, seeing what he did for a living. Something about this felt wrong.

"Are there usually this small number of you?"

"N...no," Tobias stuttered. His worry only made her feel more afraid. She gripped her bow tightly. She missed the security of her dagger that usually weighed down her clothes, making her feel safe.

"Then why..." She stopped short. They were not even in position yet, and she could hear the cart's wheels crushing into the road. She heard Tobias curse under his breath. He snuck over to where he could see the road and she followed, as quietly as she could. She could not get used to these heavy shoes and it was almost impossible to tread lightly in them.

A quiet whistle echoed, and Tobias nodded to himself.

"Care to tell me what that meant?"

"Oh." It was as though he had forgotten she was there. *Great, put me with the idiot.*

"We are going ahead anyway. They are in position. We need to watch in case we are needed." It seemed easy enough to Marian, but something did feel wrong. The cart came into view. Marian could see a man holding the reins of the horse and a younger man next to him. She guessed they were father and son, with about the right age gap. It looked like the cart was carrying wool or some sort of material.

Then Alan stepped out into the road with a sword. Marian had not even noticed he was carrying a weapon before. It looked too expensive for an outlaw to own, although they had probably stolen it. She watched as the drama unfolded.

The man slowed the horse to a stop. He whispered something to his son.

"May we pass? All we have is sheep skin. I need to deliver it. If I do not show up, the buyer will come looking for it. He is not a patient man."

"That is not our problem." Pit, a lanky man, appeared at the side of the cart. "Think he is telling the truth?"

"Well, we will have to find out." Lucas appeared on the other side. The man in the cart tried to pull on the horse's reins to get it moving again. Alan gave one swoop of his sword and the reins came away. Alan jumped up onto the horse with no effort and watched the man with a smirk.

"Please," the man begged. His son was too quiet. He did not seem frightened, more waiting for an opportunity. She watched him carefully and prepared an arrow just in case.

"Well, well," she heard Lucas say. She turned to see him holding a bag. He put his hand in and took out a few coins. "We have a couple of liars here. Do you know what we do with liars?"

Pit laughed, and then it happened in slow motion.

Marian saw a movement in the corner of her eye. She looked and noticed the son moving. He was trying to grab something from under him and threw it at Pit before Marian could react. A dagger. It sailed through the air and Marian watched as it landed on the floor just in front of Pit. His laughter stopped. He looked at the son, enraged. The boy had only tried to protect himself, what any normal person would do. If he had just let them carry out the steal, perhaps he and his father would have gotten away.

The father slapped the boy, calling him something she could not quite hear. And then Pit was next to the boy, dragging him out of the cart. The boy screamed. He was old enough to be a man but he seemed so baby faced. The father sat in the cart, staring after the boy, but did nothing. *What a coward*, Marian thought. He did not even bother standing up for his own son. Pit held the dagger the boy had thrown at his neck.

"How do you like it now? I could slice so easily and you would be dead."

He was not going to kill the boy, surely not? Just take the cart and leave them to fend for themselves. Killing was not necessary, at least give them a chance. This felt unnatural and unfair. She had to take action. Without thinking, Marian stood, and ran down to the road. She heard Tobias shout but ignored him. When she got to the road, she slowed down, taking in the action around her. She studied the situation to see what she could do.

"Marian," Alan warned.

She did not know how, instinct perhaps, but she had her bow and arrow pointed at Pit.

"He is just a boy. He was only trying to defend himself," she reasoned with him.

"Hell, he is probably embarrassed. He could not even throw it far enough to hit you."

"Not enjoying what we do, girl? This is what we do." At that, he started to slit the boy's throat.

Nobody had been watching the father. They were too busy watching Pit and the boy.

The father grabbed Marian from behind and she dropped her bow in surprise.

"Let go of my son. You kill him and I kill her."

Pit only smiled and slit the throat further. "Go ahead, by all means."

Alan yelled something but she was too focused. The man holding her was weak, old; he was not holding her very tightly. She kicked her leg back with force and he let go, cursing every word known to man. She picked up her bow and readied it. This was no place for her. She wanted nothing to do with these men. She thought these outlaws would be better than the rogues who kidnapped her, but they were just as bad. She did not belong here.

"Let the boy go. You can take the cart and everything inside but leave the boy and his father. Let them live."

"I do not take orders from you!" Pit rumbled.

"Drop the dagger, Pit." Robin's voice boomed through the forest. Marian could not even tell where he was, but relief washed over her. He was on her side. Pit dropped the dagger, confused and angry. "Now let the boy and his father go." Pit let the boy go and he ran to his father. When they did not leave, Pit roared at them and they ran until they were out of sight. "Take the cart to camp. I will meet you there later. Alan and Marian, walk with me."

#

Alice waited close to the servants' gate of the castle. Beatrice stood around the corner from her. They were waiting for Beatrice's friend, Emma, to come out of the gate from her shift in the castle. A few days ago, after Tuck had told Beatrice Marian was alright and hinted she would return, Beatrice and Alice had decided together to start investigating what was happening in the castle. They knew Gisbourne and the Sheriff were corrupt and they could not simply sit around waiting for Marian to return to them. Alice felt exhilarated that she could be useful for something and it was exciting to go on an adventure. She had met Emma a couple of times now, and thought she was a good person, but she did not know if Emma would agree to what they were going to ask of her. The castle was full of secrets and if Emma was caught, the consequences would be devastating.

Eventually, Emma walked out of the servants' gate with a group of servants finishing their shifts. She noticed Alice and Beatrice but carried on walking. They followed a few steps behind; this had to be secretive and they could not risk anyone listening in. They followed her down the streets leading home. Finally, she walked around the back of her home, and stopped. Alice and Beatrice came around the corner.

"Another favour?" It did not give Alice much confidence, but she was the only person with access, that they could trust. She had risked everything to help Alan escape gaol and Alice hoped she would help them further.

"Not a favour, but an opportunity," Beatrice explained. She had always been a friend to Emma and had helped her support her unwell son. Alice could tell Beatrice hated to ask so much of a woman already under incredible strain. They would have asked someone else, but Emma was the only one they could entrust this task with. "We need someone on the inside. We believe the Sheriff and Gisbourne are corrupt and need to find proof."

"But there is nothing you can do, even if there is proof. They are powerful."

"That is true, but the people could turn against corrupt power if they knew what was going on. There are far more ordinary people than those in power, and they need us to feed their greed," Beatrice replied.

"The choice is yours," Alice chimed in, attempting not to make it sound so drastic.

"I will do what I can, but I will not do anything that risks being discovered. My boy needs me and I cannot afford to risk that. If they are as corrupt as you say they are, I do not want to get on their bad side."

#

Marian was surprised by Robin's calmness. She could sense it was misplaced, his real emotions buried deep inside.

"That was a test," Alan said matter-of-factly.

"It was."

"You know Pit's temper. You expected him to act that way. Is that why you left? You were watching to see how we would do."

"You were going to let Pit kill the boy." Marian was suddenly angry at Robin.

Robin stopped, turning to look at Marian for the first time. For a moment, he studied her. "Marian, this is no place for you. You do not like what we do. For goodness' sake, leave. You are more trouble than you are worth. You do not belong here and you will only get in the way. You are too weak, too feminine and caring." The words stung. She could feel herself deflating more with every insult. She wanted to run; her usual coping mechanism. But she had nowhere to run to.

Robin turned to Alan. "And you. You are not the ruthless man I once thought you to be. Perhaps you are well suited for one another. Do not bother coming back to camp, either of you." He walked off, Robin seemed to do that a lot, a sign he did not like being overruled.

Marian and Alan stood side by side, staring hopelessly at the forest ahead of them.

She did not know what to say.

"What do we do now?" Alan sounded lost. He looked to Marian, as if she might know.

Finally, she realised where she belonged. "We go home, to Nottingham."

Chapter 21

Emma waited until dark to wander the corridors and spy on those inside the castle. She did not like being close to danger, but she had to do something. The halls were lit with candles and reflected a red glow on the normally grey, dull walls. Her job was the only thing that brought money into her household and she needed it to be able to look after George. He was not getting any better, but to her relief, he was not getting worse either. She could not risk getting caught.

For the past two days, she had been listening through the walls while going about her duties, but there had not even been a whisper of contempt towards the people. This was her last chance to find information, as after tonight, she promised herself she would give up. It was not worth the danger if she did not find anything out. Emma felt uneasy putting her nose into others' business; she would rather just put up with whatever the Sheriff had planned. It was the easy way out, but her conscience would not let her take the easy route.

Emma walked past the Great Hall as usual. No guards were stationed around the area, but she could hear a voice from inside. She neared the door cautiously. It definitely sounded like the Sheriff and he was not happy.

"What do you mean? There is no way she is still alive. We made sure of that. But if you are that paranoid, just go there and see for yourself. I am sure the maids will know whether she is alive or not. Find out. I am off to my chambers. Do not bother me with your silly guilt or love or whatever it is. It is becoming tedious."

Emma ran down the corridor as fast as her legs could carry her. She was too scared to stay and see who the Sheriff was talking to. She had to warn Beatrice and Alice, but there was nothing she could do. If the person was leaving now, she would have no chance of getting there first. This was dangerous enough work for her. Instead she walked home to tend on her son. She was sure Alice and Beatrice could handle themselves. She could no longer be a part of this.

"Pit would have killed that boy. How could Robin let him?" Marian could not understand what kind of man would take pleasure in such a thing. These outlaws were just as bad as Gisbourne and her uncle.

"But he stopped it," Alan replied.

"Only because I was getting in the way. Is that what you do? Kill innocent people?"

"You saw, I could not even control what was happening. I was useless. I could have stopped it myself. I could have…" Marian noticed he avoided answering the question.

"So, you used to do that, under Robin's orders?" She was disgusted.

"You have to remember. Everyone is an outlaw for a reason, most in Robin's gang are dangerous criminals – some murderers even."

"Some still are," Marian observed, feeling empty. "But what is the point?"

"Survival: they run on instinct. If they are threatened, they threaten back. It is the only way we… they know," Alan corrected himself. "Pit did not harm the boy until he threw a dagger at him. That was a threat and Pit just did what he knew – he got rid of the threat."

"But how can you justify that?"

"Outlaws, Marian," he replied tiresomely. "Please can we worry about what we are going to do now? You cannot just waltz up to the Sheriff and announce you are alive."

"The shock might kill him. Great idea," she said more seriously than she should have.

The truth was that she had tried to distract herself from thinking about what she was going to do in Nottingham, and the only way she could do that was by talking about Robin and the outlaws. And now she had to face the fact she had no clue what she might face.

They were close to Nottingham, she could sense it. She was starting to recognise the route through the forest. They stayed clear of the road, making sure nobody would recognise her. Marian did not have any way of disguising herself so she had to be extra careful. Alan stayed ahead of her, alert. It was starting to get dark.

"We should go to the manor. I know I cannot stay there, but there are clothes inside, a cloak I can disguise myself with."

"Alright, but we have to be careful. It is probably being watched. We will take a back route, stay close to me."

And suddenly they were out in the open, the forest behind them. She sighed with relief. She had originally liked the freedom of the forest, but now she was happy to be somewhere she recognised. It could never be the same as she remembered it, though. Those were distant memories now, of a fond life she had; another thing taken away from her by her uncle.

Marian let Alan lead her through the winding roads, hiding behind buildings, making sure the way ahead was clear. Marian was not scared, nor was she excited. All she wanted to do was sleep in her own bed, but she could not do that. Somehow the Sheriff and Gisbourne would find out. Where could she go to live? Another town? Perhaps have a new identity again? She knew her future would be hiding and praying that the Sheriff never found her, just what she had been doing for years in Nottingham. It was the vicious cycle of her life, it seemed. Somewhere deep inside her, she still wanted to die, but she shut it off, not letting anyone see the truth, not even herself. She silently wished for the feeling to go away, but she deserved it. For Meggy, and for the other servants she never knew, but who helped her anyway and died as a result. *They saved me for a reason. They would be so disappointed that they have died for nothing. I am nothing.*

They were now close to the manor. Marian took the lead this time, looking around the corner of a cottage, the closest building to the manor, but still a clear gap separating the buildings. She could not simply walk out into it, not knowing who might see. She looked into the manor, trying to see…

She noticed a shadow in one of the windows, Beatrice. A candle blew out and Marian's home was dark. Perhaps Beatrice was going to bed, it was almost night-time. The sun had set and there was little light left. Perhaps she could sleep in the stable with Chestnut. But then the door opened and Beatrice left. She was coming around the corner when Alan grabbed Beatrice, holding his hand to her mouth to stop her from screaming. Beatrice wriggled in his grasp. Marian approached her.

"Beatrice, it is me, Marian," she whispered. Beatrice went still. "Alan, let her go, she will not try anything." He let go and Beatrice turned and slapped him. He did not try to stop her nor did he react.

"Marian, my darling. Are you alright?" She fussed over Marian, examining her from head to toe.

"Beatrice, stop, please. I need your help. We need your help."

"You cannot be here. Gisbourne has been watching this place. We have kept it going for you, but he knows in that black heart of his, that you are not dead. I guess he will not be satisfied until he sees a body. Or perhaps he just misses you and this reminds him of you," Beatrice said in a sickly-sweet way that made Marian's stomach churn.

"Well that means we have to be extra careful. I need some clothes. Grab my cloak; I will need it to stay hidden."

"What about that outfit you had made for you? In case you ever needed it?"

"That is a great idea Beatrice, thank you." A couple of years ago, Marian had wanted to join the Sheriff's guards but Walter had refused her. She had approached a merchant and had a custom fitted armour made for her for a high price, and even higher for his secrecy. She could barely remember what it looked like as she had stored it away and never had a use for it. But it would be perfect now. It even had a cloak and hood so she could go unnoticed.

Beatrice rushed back inside to collect a few things for them. Alan turned to Marian.

"So, what is your plan?"

"I am not quite there yet," Marian replied, embarrassed for not thinking ahead. "It will work out, it has to."

"You do not need to prove that to me. I am with you no matter what."

"Why Alan? Why would you risk everything for me? I do not deserve it."

"You think so little of yourself Marian. You are so much more. You are strong and brave and clever, you stand up for what is right. You have shown me a new way of living. I have nothing left to risk, so you do not need to worry yourself about me. I, like you, can take care of myself and I choose to be here, whether you want me or not."

"But..."

"I will not question your choices, so please do not question mine."

"Sorry, I just do not understand it."

"Perhaps one day you will, but first we need a place to stay."

Beatrice returned, and gave Marian a basket full of clothes. "Now, I have an idea for that too," she replied, having overheard the conversation. Beatrice had always been an eager listener, sometimes a little too eager. She loved the gossip. "There is an abandoned cottage at the far end of the city, close to the forest. Nobody likes to live there, everyone is scared of being that close to the outside world. No one will bother you, just keep it dark and try not to attract attention.

Do you know the place I am talking about? I had better not leave, someone might be watching. If you need anything, I do my rounds to some of the folk every day. I have taken up your chores for them. They are in a bad way. Never mind, you will find out soon enough. Now off you pop. Try not to get yourselves caught." Before Marian could thank her, she rushed back inside without a glance back. Marian was ready to sleep. She led the way through the deserted streets of the night.

When they arrived, both exhausted, they collapsed onto the rotting hay beds and fell asleep straight away.

#

It was the middle of the night, but Alice could not sleep. Beatrice had informed her of Marian's return, but it unsettled her. This was not Marian's best plan, she should have stayed in the forest, at least until everything settled down here. But Alice knew she must have had no other choice. She was simply grateful that Marian was alive.

There was a thud against the door, and Alice rushed out of her quarters to see what was happening. Gisbourne stood where the front door had been forced open. Her heart raced and she panicked. This was going to be the end. Beatrice appeared next to her, and she relaxed ever so slightly.

Gisbourne looked wild, his eyes frantic and unfocused. Alice could not hint to him that Marian was alive. She had to play along. When Beatrice did not take control, Alice ran towards Gisbourne. She fell purposefully at his feet, hysterical.

"What happened to her? Please, I have to know," she wailed. "What is the point in life now Marian is gone? What will I do?"

She looked up at Gisbourne. He seemed surprised. She waited for him to speak, and then Beatrice came up beside her.

"Are you here to evict us? Please let us stay. We will serve whoever lives here," Beatrice begged. "It is all we know."

It took a minute for Gisbourne to compose himself. He seemed to like having power, especially over weak women, and this was playing in their favour. It was night, and a strange time for a visitor. He must feel guilty, Alice realised, smiling internally at his torture.

"I will allow you both to stay. I thought there was a man servant too?" He was suspicious, Alice gulped down the lump in her throat.

"We do not know what happened to him. Perhaps he suffered the same fate as poor Marian," Alice suggested meekly.

"I very much doubt that," he replied solemnly. Gisbourne did have a spark for Marian after all.

He turned and stormed back out. Alice sighed with relief.

"We are going to have to get that door fixed," Beatrice said to herself.

Chapter 22

Tobias walked along the border that separated Nottingham from the forest, staying close to the trees. He had been entrusted with an errand by Robin and he did not understand why, out of all the outlaws, he had been chosen to fulfil it. He had been wandering around for hours, having seen nothing yet. As soon as Robin had returned to camp alone, Tobias had been sent here to keep an eye on Alan and Marian from a distance. For some reason, Robin still cared about their safety, or wanted the gossip.

He had eventually caught a glimpse of Alan and Marian returning to Nottingham, sneaking through unnoticed by others. He watched as they got further out of his sight. He decided to leave them for now and stay put, just in case they returned. He sat down on the ground, as shadows stretched across the land. He rested his aching back against a tree and fell asleep.

"Hello, outlaw. It is not your day, is it? Trying to attack a poor person in Nottingham. You are a criminal and you will be punished."

Tobias opened his eyes, knots forming in his stomach. He stared up and into the glare of Gisbourne. He had never met him before, but he knew it was him. All the rumours were true. Other guards appeared around him, covered head to toe in armour. He had no chance of escaping.

Then Gisbourne laughed.

"You are a dull one, not even attempting to escape. You will have to do, though. Guards, the Sheriff will want to see this one."

#

The nightmares had returned last night. Marian started to look through the basket Beatrice had given her. Beatrice always thought of everything, she had even put in a fresh loaf of bread. Then she noticed the gear. Marian tried it on, hoping that it would still fit. She thought she would look silly in it; after all it was out of ignorance that she had bought it in the first place. But she looked down at herself and was amazed. She looked completely different. The black material hugged her body like a glove but was comfortable and moveable. It hid her chest to the point she could not tell whether she looked like a man or a woman, and the cloak and hood was the perfect size to shadow her face making it hard to even recognise herself. *I am a fighter, a warrior. I always find a way to survive, even when it seems impossible.*

"You look…" Alan was speechless for once in his life. Marian turned, embarrassed.

He looked at her in amazement. "Nice outfit. Do I have one to match?"

"No, sorry. Beatrice did put in some of your old clothes though. Here." She passed them to him.

"What is the plan today, oh wise one?"

"I think you spent too much time around Will."

"I miss them," he said suddenly.

"I miss them too," she replied, surprising herself. She had gotten to know Will and Little John and really enjoyed their company. She knew she would probably never see them again, and the darkness returned to her. She always lost friends. Just when things started to improve, something would destroy everything once again; *Story of my life.*

"I need to pay Tuck a visit, find out what is happening."

"I will come too. He did save me from the castle."

"About that, how on earth did he manage it?" She had tried to imagine how a friar, even one who had lost his faith, would be able to break a man out of gaol, when nobody else could manage it.

"Tuck claimed that he was there for my confession." He chuckled. Marian was in awe of Tuck's cunning abilities. If he did not wear the robes of a friar, nobody would ever think he could be a man of God.

"And they just let him walk in without question?"

"The Sheriff and Gisbourne had left, so they could not question it. None of them knew who Tuck was. He obviously has some talent for these things. Perhaps he could teach us a thing or two. Anyway, he snuck me out, no trouble at all. Well, we had to disarm a couple of guards." Then, seeing Marian's disapproving expression, he added: "Nothing serious. They are probably fine."

"He is more skilled than I thought," Marian wondered in awe.

#

Tobias sat in his cell in darkness. He did not know how long had passed, nor whether it was day or night. The only thing he knew for certain was that he was going to die, Gisbourne would make sure of it. He knew about Gisbourne's bloodlust for outlaws, he would get no leniency. He felt strangely at peace. He was always terrified of what others thought, especially those above him – which was practically everyone. He had never fit in as an outlaw. Tobias had been in the forest for about a year and every day was hard for him. He never found a friend, even when Robin had let him into their gang, he could not bring himself to fight or hurt anyone, so he usually got left behind, watching from a distance. He did not understand why Robin let him stay, he should have made him fend for himself as he was absolutely no use to the outlaws.

Tobias thought about his family; his father who never cared much for him, being the youngest and the runt of the family. His mother loved him but she was always swayed to his father's will. His two older brothers were nasty to him as well. They were the reason he was now an outlaw. Rufus, his oldest brother, five years his superior and always liked to gloat about it, had stolen goods from a baker and he had managed to persuade his brother, Henry, and his father that Tobias had stolen them. When the guards came knocking, they believed the story and tried to arrest Tobias. His mother managed to get Tobias out and told him to run before the guards could arrest him. He had not looked back since. But he was still no outlaw. He did not know how he had survived this long. It did not matter anyway, as he would soon hang. He curled up into a ball. He did not want to die.

#

Marian and Alan took to the streets in search of Tuck. As long as they did not bump into Gisbourne, they would be safe. Even so, they stayed to the shadows and the crowds.

As they made their way through the market, Marian noted it was market day. She had lost track of time in the forest and not even noticed the days passing. They walked through the unusually empty and neglected marketplace. Market day had always attracted not just the people of Nottingham, but traders and people from further towns and villages. It was renowned as being one of the biggest markets in England and Marian had always found pleasure in the way people came together in one place to celebrate the tradition.

The usual crowds were reduced to a few small stalls selling little more than junk. Marian felt a pang of guilt for these people. As per usual, she had not thought about anyone but herself nor of the consequences to the people of Nottingham for having such a cruel and unforgiving man as their Sheriff. She had left them to his wrath, and she had never imagined it would leave such a bad impact on the city. Marian used to find it a joy, walking through the market, watching as people sold their spare goods to help others out at reduced prices. Now, Marian's heart sank, seeing the devastating influence of such a powerful, merciless man, her uncle.

They reached the stocks by the end of the wall that separated the two sides of the market. This was the one area Marian had not liked. She could not stand the idea of the stocks but now they seemed a kind punishment compared to her uncle's theatrical displays. Shame was a horrible thing to see in a man's eyes but at least they would live and have the chance to regain their dignity someday. The Sheriff was murdering people. It did not matter the crime, nobody deserved to die as a result.

Marian led the way towards the tavern and, at first, she could not see Tuck. She peered into the tavern, not wanting to go inside, and found to her surprise that he was nowhere to be seen. She heard her name and panicked for a moment, before noticing Tuck, looking around from the side of the building. He vanished around the corner, and Marian followed, Alan staying close behind. She eventually found Tuck hidden in the shadows around the back of the tavern.

"I was hoping you would show up at some point." He sounded different. His speech was clearer and he looked more alive than he had been in a very long time. He was sober, Marian realised. She should be happy for him, but it unsettled her; something had forced him to sober up. "Why are you here? The Sheriff has spies everywhere. It is not a good place to be. You need to leave, now."

"Tuck, there is nowhere else for us to go."

"Well a lot has changed since you left."

"I could see. The market square is almost empty. What happened?"

"It is the Sheriff and his puppy Gisbourne. They have increased the taxes so much that nobody can afford to live. Those who cannot pay end up in the gaol. Some have even been hung as an example. The people are afraid."

"I should have killed him. I just froze... I..." If Marian had just used the skills she had taught herself, then her uncle may have been dead by now and it would be over. But she could not go back, she could not change anything.

"There is a gathering in the courtyard this afternoon. I do not know what it is about, but it is bound to be more bad news. The Sheriff has ordered that each household must attend. There will be a big crowd, there is no threat of being discovered. Feel free to come along to see for yourselves the state of the city. Now leave, we cannot attract attention." He turned to Alan. "When the Sheriff and Gisbourne returned, they knew you had escaped and they were not happy. They are on the lookout for a friar, and I need to keep a low profile."

"Stay with us, Tuck. We are in the abandoned home near the forest," Alan suggested.

"No, I need to be out here. I will tell you if I hear anything of use to you. I will see you later at the gathering."

#

Tobias heard a clanging of chains and looked up. His cell opened and he strained his eyes to try to see who was in the cell with him. Gisbourne.

He cowered away from him, but Gisbourne was strong. He grabbed his ankle and dragged him from the cell, unable to get a grip on anything. Finally, he stopped and let go. Before Tobias could kick away, he was lifted by two guards and placed on a table, where Gisbourne locked his hands and ankles into chains. Tobias had hoped it would be a quick death, but this was going to be much worse.

"Please, let me die. Just kill me now," he begged, unable to stop himself. He had never been very brave, and he could not help but pray for mercy.

"You really are a coward!" Gisbourne smirked, holding back a laugh.

Another voice came, one he could not put a face to. "Do you want me to start?" The voice was slimy and sent a chill through his body. He must be the torturer.

"Go ahead. Shall we see what information we can get from him?" Gisbourne stepped back so Tobias could not see him anymore, and the torturer came into view.

"This will hurt, outlaw." He spat at Tobias. He held up a small knife, sharp enough to slice through armour even.

"We can stop this before it gets messy. You just have to tell me what you know," Gisbourne's voice came from somewhere in the room.

"What do you want to know?"

"Do you belong to a gang?"

"No," he whispered. There was a pause, and the torturer made a thin slice on Tobias's leg. He gasped with the sudden pain.

"Who is your leader?"

"I do not have a leader. I am alone."

"If you keep lying to us, it will only get worse. We can stop it if you tell the truth."

Tobias closed his mouth, stopping the screams building in his throat. He looked into Gisbourne's eyes, back in his view. They would not stop torturing him, even if he told them the truth. He did not open his mouth again.

#

Before attending the gathering, Marian returned to the cottage to collect weapons. She found the dagger Beatrice had left her in the basket and concealed it within her outfit. There was also the short sword that she had practiced with, and finally Marian slung her bow behind her back, with the cloak covering it. Even if she would not use it, it made her feel safer, knowing she could defend herself should the need arise. Alan, as usual, had his weapon of choice, a sword, and she suspected he also hid a few daggers. He did not wear any protective gear, but she was certain he could handle himself.

They followed the crowd into the castle courtyard. It felt strange for Marian to be on the receiving end of the gathering; when Walter was alive, she used to stand close to him, though hidden from view, when he addressed the people. Alan followed her silently and closely, as a reassurance that everything was alright, even though she knew it was far from that.

"We do not have to do this," Alan whispered to her, before going through the gate to the courtyard. She knew he was only trying to protect her, but she had to see what was happening. In a way, she also wanted to see the Sheriff, because it all still felt like a nightmare and she could not quite get her head around the fact he was actually here. She needed to see the truth and stop lying to herself. She ignored Alan and continued to follow the crowd in.

Marian immediately noticed the gallows with a rope attached, and an executioner waiting. Walter had never enjoyed public execution, but she remembered a few occasions when he had been forced to attend one in his own city; one of which by a lord who wanted revenge on an outlaw for killing his livestock. Marian used to agree to the punishment of criminals who committed crimes such as murder, but she had never approved of killing as a punishment; that made the rule makers just as bad as the murderers themselves. She hoped it would not be an innocent life going to waste today. She was not sure if she would be able to bear watching such an horrific act. She did not have a taste for bloodshed unless it was necessary.

The crowd around them came to a standstill and Marian looked back, feeling like she was being herded. To her relief, the gates remained open; the crowds being so overwhelmingly large that they spilled out into the surrounding area. Her attention returned to the castle steps as she heard the great doors creak open. And there they were.

The Sheriff walked out first, smiling a wicked grin of victory. Gisbourne followed and Marian noticed how tired he looked. Even at a distance, she could see the greyness surrounding his eyes and he walked slowly as if he had just been through a battle and the adrenaline had worn off. She smiled inwardly; at least he was suffering, though his smug grin made her want to send an arrow through his heart.

"My people. I have great news for you all. I have been tiresomely working to get you what you want. Your taxes are not wasted. Myself and the King are grateful for your cooperation. I am a sheriff for the people. I know you have been suffering greatly. But I have a treat for you." Marian could not believe the nonsense coming out of the Sheriff's mouth, trying to excuse himself for the woes he was causing. "Gisbourne has captured an outlaw on the borders. The beast was attempting to attack the lovely people of Nottingham, but with the help of my guards, Gisbourne managed to capture the demon before he struck. And he is here for you to receive, to see the whites of his eyes before he dies."

Guards streamed out with a man in the centre. Marian rose onto her tiptoes to see who it was, and she recognised him. Alan gasped in shock beside her and breathed 'Tobias'.

Marian could not believe it. Tobias must have happened across the worst person an outlaw could ever cross paths with. He was only a young man, not yet used to an outlaw's lifestyle and a bit of an outcast, even for an outlaw. His clothes were torn and Marian suspected he had been tortured for information on Robin and his gang, or maybe even about Arthur. Tobias looked terrified, searching the crowds, probably hoping somehow Robin had found out about his capture and come to save him. Marian shook her head. Robin would not take the risk to show up in such a place just to save one man, even one of his own.

The drums started. Marian's uncle had always been one for dramatics. She watched him as he acted like an excited child, waiting for a treat. Then Marian's instincts kicked in. She could not just let Tobias die. He had not caused her any problems, and for all she knew, he could be an innocent. Either way, he was surely more innocent than Gisbourne, or worse, the Sheriff. She could not stand idly aside and watch him die. She refused to see the hope leave him as he knew nobody was coming to save him.

Then he dropped, and Marian had let go of the dagger, and it was flying towards the rope where Tobias dangled.

Chapter 23

The courtyard turned into chaos. The townspeople gasped in horror as Tobias fell to the stage, choking and spluttering. Everyone surged towards the gates to get away. In the panic, Marian heard the Sheriff order his archers to shoot, sending arrows into the bodies of innocents. Marian could feel Alan trying to pull her away with the crowds, but she held her ground. Her focus was solely on Tobias. The confusion in the guards' faces was replaced by the desire to fulfil their leader's orders. They started towards Tobias with swords drawn.

Marian ignored Alan's protests and ran forwards, pushing her way through the people, even shoving some aside. She prepared an arrow and let it loose, the guard closest to Tobias screaming in pain as the arrow protruded from his leg. Her aim was to maim any threats, but never to kill. She could not cope with any more blood on her hands, already feeling the guilt eating away at her soul. Marian heard Alan close in behind her, and the scraping of his sword as it came out of his belt. Suddenly he was ahead of her and he jumped with ease onto the gallows stage. He fought against the few guards focused on Tobias, and Marian took the moment to take in the scene unfolding around her.

Bodies littered the floor; it was a massacre. Arrows were still flying through the air as the crowds dispersed from the courtyard. There were not many people left, soon the guards would only see Marian, Alan and Tobias.

"We need to go now!" Marian warned and Alan pulled Tobias up, jumping off the stage as they ran for the gates.

The guards charged towards them, and Marian ran as fast as her legs would allow.

They were almost at the gates.

"They are getting closer. We need to stop them," she shouted, and Alan stopped in his tracks, turning to face the guards. "Run!" he yelled to Marian and Tobias but Marian refused to let him get himself killed. She looked up and saw the metal gate pulled up. It was attached to some rope that had been wound up, if she could just cut it…

"No. There is another way. Get past the gates," Marian called. They all backed up quickly, facing the guards who were closing in on them. Marian prepared her bow one last time, and an arrow flew above their heads.

"What are you…" Alan started, until he realised what she had done. The arrow pierced a piece of rope and the gates slammed shut, separating them from the enemies.

"Now run!" Marian led and she could hear Alan and Tobias hot on her heels, though she did not look to check. They ran all the way to the cottage through back routes and around in circles, slowing down the further they got and the more certain they were that they were no longer being followed. Close to the cottage they were cautious to ensure they would not be seen by anyone. They waited in the shadows until the sun was beginning to go down and they crept into the cottage.

"Well I was not expecting that!" Tobias leaned against the door, catching his breath.

"I just knew I was going to die, and then suddenly I was free. But why?"

"Anyone would have done it. Why did none of the outlaws come to save you?" Marian had thought they at least looked out for their own. Although now, she was beginning to understand they had no morals whatsoever.

"That is not our way. We look out for ourselves."

"Every man for himself." Marian was disgusted by this belief, that no one would risk their own lives to save another. Thinking about it, that was probably why they never thought of ridding themselves of Gisbourne; they did not dare risk their own lives when they could make excuses instead.

"Well we are different," Alan explained to Tobias. "Marian and I have principles and know the difference between right and wrong. I did not know I still had it in me, but now I know I am destined for another life than being an outlaw. I cannot live by their selfish ways anymore."

Marian looked at Tobias and noticed a change in him. He appeared older and… surprised?

#

Tobias could not get over the fact that anyone would risk their lives to save him, let alone a woman. He had not done anything to deserve her help, nor Alan's. Why had they saved him? He did not even know them that well. Tobias was a new outlaw, having been punished for his brother's crimes. He had happened across Robin's gang and they had let him become part of the gang, though he had yet to prove himself. Being a leader prevented Robin from thinking about individual lives and turned him into a man of little cares, but that of survival. That was what Little John had told him anyway. He needed to head back to Robin to tell him what had happened, but he no longer felt loyal to him. Robin did not stand for anything, whereas Marian and Alan had an unspoken code. They saved him, even if he did not deserve it. He owed them his life. Robin only lived to survive; he did not care what he did, what he made of himself. He wasted his life by surviving, and Tobias had been doing the exact same thing. What was the point in living when your life was worth nothing?

"I really do not know how to repay you. You saved me and I owe you my life. First, I have to return to Robin. He will want to know what the Sheriff is doing to outlaws. Then I will return. In the gaol, Gisbourne had been torturing innocent people who did not deserve it. Not for information or obedience, but for the sake of it. I understood why I would receive such punishment, being on the run from the law. I was tortured for what seemed like information but every time I gave an answer, he would call me a liar, wanting to see me suffer and did not care if he got any information or not. There were so many crammed into that small space. They need some hope like you, Marian. People would follow you. I mean, you already had Alan on your side, and now you have me as well. For that I thank you."

As Tobias was about to open the door, Alan asked: "Why were you here? Robin made it clear that we were not part of his gang."

"Because he asked me to look out for you both." He turned and left without another word.

#

Marian could not comprehend anything that had happened today. She did not understand why Robin would send Tobias to look out for her. She wanted nothing to do with his gang. They did whatever they wanted and ignored the consequences. She needed to right her wrongs the best she could and being in his gang would have only made things worse. A weight fell upon her, and her energy ebbed from the events of the day. She was too tired to waste energy on such a trivial thing. She would probably never see him again anyway.

Collapsing onto the hay, she sighed.

"I cannot watch the Sheriff kill the entire city. Someone needs to take a stand against him, give the people some hope."

There was a knock at the door, and Marian and Alan froze. They looked at each other warily, and Alan cautiously peered around the door. Seeing his body relax, Marian stood, wondering who it could be. Alan opened the door slightly and Tuck walked in, shutting the door carefully behind him.

Marian sat back down. She watched Tuck in the ebbing light of the day and waited for him to speak.

"What you did today, that was impressive. I have never seen someone get the better of the Sheriff and Gisbourne before. I mean, a few have tried, but they all ended up dead within a matter of seconds. That was something else! I know that this is what my true purpose in life is supposed to be. I can hear destiny calling to me. What is the plan?" He seemed so chirpy and dreamy, very unlike himself.

Marian was baffled. "How did you know I would save Tobias?"

"I knew you were born to be a leader. I have always known it. God, or fate, granted me a dream of a woman who would give the people hope. You are that woman, Marian. Look around, you are building yourself an army. Many more will join you if you reach out to them. Start small and grow, then we can attack at the source of the cruelty." Tuck had so much belief in her. Was he right? Marian had never before thought of herself as a leader, and she did not want to lead men to their deaths. She would not be able to handle the pressure. It dawned on her that this must be how Robin felt every day, weighing up whose lives were worth more than others.

"I am no leader."

"Then a team. We will work together, each of us willing to do whatever it takes. I have had years of seeking out truths, I can be the eyes and ears. Marian, you can inspire the people, be the face of the revolution. Alan, you are skilled in weaponry and perhaps you could even get some outlaws on our side. This can work, I know it. You just have to believe in yourself and what we are trying to achieve. I know that this is right, and I know you do too."

"But how? What can we do? He is the Sheriff. He has guards, and Gisbourne. We would never be able to get to him. And we cannot stay here forever. They will find us. They must already be searching, soon they will figure it out. They will learn somehow that I am alive and then we will all be in danger. We cannot be found out."

"The King has to officially deem someone the Sheriff. Since Walter came into the position, no one has been the true High Sheriff. We need to fight, in whatever ways we can, against this oppression."

Alan stepped in. "We will take to the forest. There are abandoned barns and cottages close by, places outlaws have used in winters past, where no one lives anymore. We can deal with outlaws better than we can deal with trained guards."

"Then we head there. Do you have a specific place in mind?" Marian asked. "I do."

They all grabbed as much as they could carry and left immediately, before any guards could come snooping around. It was night-time but Marian was not afraid. Tuck was right, this felt natural. This would give her a reason to live, a purpose, as Tuck had put it. But she was still not sure whether she could inspire people to join them, she had to try to fight against the oppression of the Sheriff. There was a plan coming together in her mind, but she had to do this alone. She could not risk anyone else's lives.

Tuck and Marian followed Alan through the forest, making sure to stay close, as they could not see very far ahead in the darkness that clung to the trees. It was not a long walk, close to the town, but far enough not to be targeted by the Sheriff.

Alan stopped a little ahead of them and Marian saw it. An old, rotting, wooden barn but it was good enough for their use. There would be enough space to train, and it was surrounded by tall trees making the barn blend in. They made themselves at home, laying out some blankets on old hay and slept.

Chapter 24

Marian watched the sky through the crack in the wood above. It was beginning to rain and she could feel splashes of water on her face. She could not stop thinking about those bodies of innocents, the pointless massacre that the Sheriff had ordered. She needed to see it all for herself. She waited until the first signs of daylight and arose silently. If Alan or Tuck woke up, they would refuse to let her go alone. She concealed her weapons and left quickly before they noticed.

Keeping to the shadows, there were no crowds to hide within, but every now and then Marian would notice someone peering out of a window, afraid of what the Sheriff might do next. It would be quiet today; the people were mourning. Marian had not allowed herself to think of it too much. She had hoped it were a bad dream, that there would be no bodies littering the castle courtyard. She prayed inwardly that they were just wounded, but she knew better.

As she approached the gates, Marian saw the true atrocity of the massacre. There were at least a dozen bodies, mainly women, scattered across the ground. The rain was heavier now, with puddles of blood flowing around the victims. The Sheriff had not even thought to clear up. He had probably left the bodies as a reminder to the people, to strike fear into their souls. What struck Marian as most odd was that there were no guards out patrolling. It was eerily silent. Marian wondered if this had been her uncle's plan all along, to send arrows pouring down on innocents, and she had given him an excuse to take the blame away from himself. Of course, he would claim they were killed by accident as the guards had tried to catch those who freed the prisoner, but he was hiding his true motives.

There was movement in the windows of the castle and Marian hid around a corner by the stables. She hugged her cloak around her, shielding her from the rain blowing into her face. Gisbourne emerged from the castle. Tuck had told her Gisbourne now had his own place away from the castle. Why had he stayed at the castle overnight then? Gisbourne looked wearier and paler than the day before, and he did not look happy. She wondered if a small part of him really had loved her, and he was still mourning her.

Gisbourne made his way through the bodies, ignoring their presence. One of the bodies, he even stepped over; no remorse for the dead. He was making his way directly towards her. She hid behind a pillar and slowly moved to the outer side as he walked into the stables. She was at risk of being seen if anyone else stepped into the courtyard, but she could not let Gisbourne see her.

Her pulse quickened and she tried to quiet her breathing. He was so close to her that if she reached around, she would be able to touch him. She listened as he prepared his horse, and she looked desperately for a way out. The stables ended after the next pillar, if she could just run, she would make it around the side of the stables and the wall would hide her. She peered around the pillar, noticing Gisbourne had his back to her, trying to saddle the horse.

This was her chance. She ran as fast as she could, past the last pillar and around the corner.

She heard a whoosh as Gisbourne turned. She closed her eyes, praying he had not seen her.

"Gisbourne," the Sheriff called, his voice echoing around the vast courtyard. "Where are you going? You need to clear this up."

"I am going home. I have helped you enough. Get one of your other servants to do the dirty work."

"You hear me? I said clean it up. I am your ruler, you do as I say. Oh," the Sheriff sneered, "you are still mad at me about Marian." She froze. Why was Gisbourne mad at the Sheriff? He had gone along with the plan to get her killed.

"She could have been mine." Gisbourne's tone had changed. He sounded angry. "You forced me to take her life away. There were other ways."

"You do not realise what an evil little swine she was. You are a better man without her."

"You mean I am more obedient without her. I could have had a life with her. I could have forced her. Surely that would have been crueller than letting her die. You know how persuasive I can be."

"No." The Sheriff cut Gisbourne off. "I will give you this day. Go home, get some sleep. You are not acting like yourself. Come back tomorrow. I do not want the bodies moulding in my courtyard. I will get some of my guards to clean it up. They can burn the bodies. These sheep do not deserve to be given back to their families. It is their punishment." He made the noise of a sheep as he returned to the castle, laughing at his own quip.

"None of this is yours. Even your title is false," Gisbourne muttered to himself, and Marian just about managed to hear. Had he really lost faith in the Sheriff? She could only hope. Even Gisbourne knew that the Sheriff had no right to the title.

Gisbourne rode his horse out of the courtyard. She had a clear view of the gate, she could get out, but she would not leave these victims to be burned like witches or heathens. After checking the coast was clear, Marian snuck into the stables and noticed a small cart and a horse. If she could get the bodies into the cart, she could lead the horse out and get away, but she had to do it unnoticed.

"What are you doing?" A small voice came from behind her. Marian whirled to see a stable boy, and the last piece of her puzzle came together.

"I am so sorry," Marian whispered, and before he could reply she punched him hard enough to knock him out. She had never hurt anyone with her bare hands before. She ignored her bruising knuckles as she took his over clothes off him. She removed her cloak, placing it on top of the little horse she was going to use, then put on the stable boy's outfit over her own attire. The stable boy was not much smaller than her and the clothes would do to blend in. She had to be quick, in case anyone came outside.

Marian moved the horse close to a body. With regret, Marian looked down at the victim; a young woman, with an arrow protruding from her chest. Marian's stomach lurched, but she took a big gulp to steady herself. She had to do this. It was for the victims, she had to forget herself and get on with it. As carefully as she could, Marian hauled the woman onto the food cart and the next, and the next, until most had been collected. She looked down at herself, covered in blood.

The last two bodies were men, quite large men she knew she did not have the energy to move. With one last look back at the scene, she held onto the horse's reins and led the cart through the town.

As she progressed towards the forest, Marian noticed a crowd building up behind her. They were all staring at her. She was covered in blood, and the overclothes she had stolen from the stable boy were ripped and ruined, revealing her soldier-like outfit beneath. They started asking questions, desperate to know the truth.

"Who are you?"

"Are those the bodies from the courtyard?"

"My wife?"

"My daughter?"

The voices were building, and Marian did not want to attract attention. She stepped forward and took a deep breath. This was the time to see if the people would listen to her, as Tuck had told her.

"I could not save the victims of the brutal attack yesterday. All I can give you is their bodies, so that you can grieve. The Sheriff was going to burn them without letting the families mourn their dead. I offer you back your dead. The Sheriff is terrorising us all. I will not stand by helpless and let him do this. I promise I will not stop fighting until we have a leader that inspires loyalty, not fear."

"You were there yesterday. You saved that outlaw. You caused these deaths."

"That outlaw is a good man. I taught him that he should have something to fight for. He is an ordinary human, just like any of us. He has seen hardship too. No man deserves to die for his past actions, everyone deserves a second chance at life. I believe the Sheriff would have found a way to justify the killings no matter what had taken place yesterday. Do not trust anything he says. These bodies are my promise to you. If I can find a way, I will. I will do my best to stop him hurting any others, innocent or otherwise. Nobody deserves to die as a punishment. I will take the cart to an old burial ground at the edge of the forest, if you wish you can bury your dead there. I will have some of my people guarding it, including a friar to see off the dead the right way. Please deal with this discreetly or the Sheriff will find out and punish you all. If you need me, follow this path and you will find myself or one of my own. I am putting my trust in you. If you do not trust me, you can tell the Sheriff where I can be found, and I can die for it. It is entirely up to you." Before anyone could question her further, Marian continued on her way to the burial ground at the outskirts of Nottingham.

Chapter 25

"Marian."

Marian was on her way back to the barn when she heard it again.

"Marian," a whisper in the trees. She recognised the voice but could not put a name to it. She turned and it had vanished again. Little John stepped into the open.

"Little John?" Marian was almost speechless. She had never expected to see him again.

"I need to ask a favour. No one can know, not even Alan."

"What do you need?" She believed Little John to be a good man at heart and wanted to see if she could help. She could not deny she was curious as to what she could ever do for him that he could not do himself.

"Promise to speak to no one of this."

"I promise. I do not have long. I need to return to Alan soon before he worries too much."

"A woman named Rose and her daughter, Emeline, live in Nottingham. I want you to give them a new start elsewhere. Please, I cannot have them live here any longer. I want them to be happy."

Marian understood and she knew not to question him. "I will do as you say. I have money they can use to start a new life and I will prepare transport for them. They will have to go through the forest."

"I will protect them in their journey. Do not tell them about me. Please, you do not know what grief it will bring them." They must be the family that he had left behind. He must have been an outlaw for many years as she had never met Little John in Nottingham, and it would be hard to miss him. Marian wondered what had forced him to become an outlaw and leave his family to fend for themselves. It must have been really bad to warrant him never even finding a way to tell his family he was alive.

"I will bring them to this spot before dark."

"I will be waiting. Thank you, Marian. You are too good." *No, I am not.*

"Where have you been?" Alan asked, the concern clear in the wavering of his voice. "You are covered in blood, are you hurt?"

"It is not mine. I stopped the bodies from being burned and gave them back to the people." Marian did not want to explain the details, she would rather forget. She took off the ruined over clothes, dropping them in a corner. Luckily, they had collected most of the blood and her own clothes were intact. It had finally stopped raining, but there was a thin mist in its place, with the rain water slowly rising in a steam, like the dampening of a fire.

Marian had wanted to sort out Little John's errand as quickly as possible, but she knew Alan would act like this. He was too protective over her, not giving her any space to do what she had to do.

"The Sheriff will find out," Alan warned.

"I do not care. They deserved to be able to bury their dead." She turned to Tuck, who had been patiently observing. "I told them of the burial site on the outskirts of Nottingham. It would be a comfort to them if you were there."

"You spoke to the people?" Tuck sounded curious.

"Yes, a few of them. They blamed me for everything."

"Did you explain yourself?"

"Yes, but I do not think they trust me. I left before they could question me any further."

"You should come with me."

"No," she replied. "They would not want me there. I am the one who started this, and I cannot make it right. I cannot bring back the dead."

"You can show them how fearless you are. Be seen in public, let them talk about you. Let word get to the Sheriff about you. Not the real you, of course; just a stranger rallying the people against the Sheriff. I think he could do with some fear."

"The Sheriff does not get frightened."

"Perhaps, perhaps not. Small steps first, remember?"

"We could get to Gisbourne easier though." Marian revelled in his internal pain.

"That is more like it," Tuck replied encouragingly. He had been right about Marian all along. She was going to be the one to save the people, or at least die trying.

"I saw him at the castle." She continued when she noticed Alan's shocked expression. "He did not see me, Alan. I was careful. I have the upper hand now. He is tortured by my death."

"Then use it," Tuck replied.

Alan stepped forward, blocking her way out. "No. You are not putting yourself in danger again."

"I have to do this. You cannot stop me. Alan, are you coming with us?" Marian replied.

"Of course, that is what I meant. You are not invincible, Marian. I just wish you had told me where you were going earlier. I could have helped. I thought this would be different than Robin's gang."

Marian was appalled by his accusation. She was nothing like Robin. She was not fearless like he was, and she certainly was not as badly tempered as him either. She could not see it herself, but it threw her off. She could not stand Robin. She had come to the conclusion that Robin was a careless man, hiding behind his outlaw gang. He did not stand for anything or do anything worthwhile with his life. "I am sorry. I will tell you next time. It was just something I had to do alone."

"We are a team, Marian. We have to work together," he said, calmer.

"I had to see for myself. Take in that everything is my fault. I have full blame and that is not something you can just fix. Nothing can make it right. I caused their deaths by acting on impulse and not thinking. Hell, I *am* like Robin then! I take it all back. I am a scheming, horrid person who takes pleasure in other people's downfalls and does not care about the consequences. I may as well be a criminal, an outlaw, who goes around stealing and killing without a thought. Breaking every rule because you can, not out of necessity or to make a stand against something, but because, why not?!" She had taken it too far, but she could not help herself. She turned away, embarrassed by what she had just said. She had not meant it to come out that way, so cruel and unforgiving. She closed her eyes and took a deep breath, trying to relax. Alan would hate her forever for what she had just said. She felt hands go around her waist and she opened her eyes, surprised. Alan held her close and whispered in her ear:

"I just want you to be safe. I cannot keep you safe if you do not tell me things. I would have let you go, I just cannot lose you."

Marian's heart faltered. She had never seen it before, but Alan loved her. She was so confused, she had never thought of him in that way, yet here they were. She did not know whether this was what love felt like, or if he was just a friend to her. Her whole life had just become a lot more complicated.

At some point Tuck had left them, and now he came around the corner. He must have heard her outburst. She had shouted loud enough. She straightened up and moved away from Alan suddenly, feeling vulnerable.

"Should we go then?" Tuck asked, and she was the first out of the barn, suddenly in need of some fresh air to cool her blushing cheeks.

#

Tuck was unused to consoling people. Long ago, part of his work with God had been to give people hope, when they had nothing else left. To help them reach out to God whose wish it had been to ruin their lives. But now it felt wrong, as though he were lying to them. If God had planned this, why would he want the people to suffer? Why did the rich, powerful folk get everything and the poor get nothing? Even the idea of God disgusted him now.

Nobody should have the power to take people's lives before their time. How was this helping the people become better? He could think of no reason for such cruelty. Yet all he knew was how to console those who had lost everything. He hoped these people would not see right through him, that he was giving them false hope he did not believe in anymore.

"God hears your prayers. He will answer them." He doubted God would listen to the prayers of the poor. God had made a deal with the devil; the Sheriff. Marian had to be the one to make things right. She was the only real hope, not God.

"Heaven was ready to accept your mother." Was there even such a thing called heaven now that God had betrayed them all?

"God understands your pain. It will make you stronger and you will find a way back into the light." He was speaking in riddles he no longer understood but were still engrained in his soul from years of worship. Saying these words of God felt blasphemous. Even doubting God was treasonous and he was doing far worse than that. Even saying the word made him cringe. If there was a God, Tuck would surely end up in Hell for this, along with every other thing he had said about God that he did not believe anymore.

#

Marian waited out of sight, watching Tuck speak his supportive words to the families of the dead. She had not expected many to turn up, but she had misinterpreted things again. That seemed to be a common theme today. Alan stood next to Marian quietly, lingering a little too close for comfort, considering the moment they had shared. She did not know how to act around him anymore.

There was a commotion between Tuck and one of the mourners. Alan pushed her forward. She looked back at him, not wanting to look into the eyes of the victims of her carelessness.

"Marian, the people need to see you. Go, be a leader. I will be here if you need me." Then he vanished into the trees. He seemed back to his usual self and she was grateful, it was one less thing she had to worry about right now. She turned to the people in front of her, some were looking at her, but she avoided their lingering stares. She did not want to see the hate in their eyes. She walked over to Tuck to see what was going on.

"The other bodies were brought back. I need to mourn my husband." It was an older woman with wrinkles on her face. She fiddled with a cheap necklace around her neck, clearly distraught. Marian stood next to Tuck, who was struggling to find an explanation. He looked to her and she spoke honestly:

"I could not get all the victims out before the castle awoke. Your husband had to be left behind. If I could have got him out, I would have." Marian's chest tightened with guilt. She should have tried to get the other two out. It was not fair on the families. It was just another mistake to add to her growing list.

"Thank you." Marian looked up, surprised. The old woman looked sincere. The tears had stopped falling and she was genuinely grateful. "I know you tried. I do not agree with those that accuse you of causing these deaths. The Sheriff is wicked and cruel, who knows what goes on in that evil mind of his! You have done the best you can. At least my husband had lived a life. His sacrifice has birthed a hero. You will save us. I have faith." She nodded to Marian, turned and left. The woman had faith in her. It was a great weight to burden; to give the people hope instead of fear. Perhaps it was possible. Marian could not let down all these people.

Marian held back tears, trying not to think about the dead before her. They were hers to live with forever. And poor Walter, the first victim of her uncle's reign of terror over Nottingham. She wished she could have buried him, she imagined an unmarked grave at the edge of the burial ground. *That is where Walter will rest*, she decided. These people all had a place to grieve. For her to grieve, Walter did not have to physically be there. The memories of him were enough.

When the area was clear, Marian picked up a small flower, walked over to the empty corner, and placed it there.

"Walter," she whispered, tears falling to the soil below her. "I miss you. I wish I had seen you more. Perhaps I could have saved you. I know you did not agree with me when I put myself in danger, but it is the right thing to do. I have to find a way to stop him, both of them. Gisbourne and the Sheriff will pay, I promise that. I vow to you that I will keep your memory alive through myself. I will make Nottingham a peaceful, happy place once more. That will be your legacy. I love you forever."

She stepped back, drying her eyes. The man who called himself Sheriff was not her uncle anymore. He was not entitled to it and from now on he was of no relation to her. She would not let him get to her anymore. It was time to let go of the past.

She turned her back to the unmarked grave, with the lonely, wilting flower, and walked away. Tuck and Alan had been stood at the edge of the forest, their backs turned to give her some privacy. Tuck turned to her as she approached and said cheerfully:

"See, you are already giving the people hope for a better future. You are a true leader. A revolution has begun."

For the first time, she truly believed in herself. "I know what we need to do next, but first, I need to do something for a friend. I promised them I would not tell anyone about it. It will put me in no danger and I will meet you at the barn before dark."

Alan was about to protest, but Tuck put a hand on his shoulder to stop him.

"Do what you have to do, Marian." Tuck knew when Marian meant business.

#

It had taken some time, and led to many dead ends, before Marian had finally found someone who knew Rose and her daughter Emeline. They lived in a tiny room in the slums of Nottingham. Most of the homes here were made of wood, with little protection from draft. She had lived such a privileged life, while others froze in their own homes. She knocked on the rotting door. Moments later it creaked open, and a woman peered her head around.

"Can I help you?" Her small voice matched her appearance; she was too thin.

"Are you Rose?"

"Yes, what do you want?"

"I am here to help you."

"Are you the woman they are talking about? The one who is going to save us?"

"Yes. Would you let me in?" It was Marian's burden – they all thought she was their saviour, but she would more likely be their downfall. She had already led her uncle here, it was her responsibility to get rid of him. The woman opened the door and shut it as soon as Marian was inside. She felt awkward, there was no place to sit, so she stood by the door.

Emeline, who looked about ten years old, sat on the bed of hay, curious. Marian imagined Little John had last seen his daughter when she was no more than a baby. She did not know how he coped without knowing if they were safe for all this time, whether they had forgotten him and moved on.

"How do you know who I am?"

"I heard from a friend that you need help. Please, I promised not to say anything and I cannot break that vow."

"Forgive me, but how can you help us?" It sounded like she had been promised things before, but at a price. She had lost all hope in the world.

"I have money and safe passage for you both to start a new life, away from all this."

"This is my home. It was my husband's home, long ago. He may be dead but perhaps he will return. I do not want to leave."

Marian had already guessed, but now she was certain; this was Little John's family. "I will tell you one thing. Your husband is alive, but he cannot return. He lives in your daughter, though, in her eyes." Rose looked stunned. She approached Marian.

"You know my husband. He told you to do this." She was crying as she whispered to make sure her daughter could not hear. "We will come with you. There is nothing left here."

Marian opened Rose's hand and placed a purse in it. Rose looked down, more tears trailing down her cheeks but now she was smiling. "Thank you. You are our blessing and we will not forget your generosity. What is your name? I will pray for your health every day. It is not much, but it is all I have."

"Thank you," Marian replied. To so many people, belief was all they had, and even though she did not believe in prayer, she knew this was the most generous gift she could have ever received. She was at peace with herself, if just for this moment. She felt good and if she died today, she would die a happy woman; to have saved this family from the wrath of the Sheriff and offer them a new life, as Walter had once done the same for her. He was looking down on her after all.

Marian escorted Rose and Emeline to the horse and cart she had bought from a merchant on her way. She led them to the place where she knew Little John would be waiting in the shadows.

"You are safe now. Your journey will not bring any danger. I have made sure of it. Good luck." Marian watched as they left, and she did not see Little John again, but she could see Rose looking into the shadows, knowing he was there, somewhere.

To Marian's surprise, when she returned to the barn, Alan and Tuck did not question where she had been. She did not have much time until her plan would be in motion. She sat beside them and told them of the mission for tonight.

Chapter 26

"Gisbourne," Marian whispered. She stood next to his bed, as he slept fitfully. She revelled in his pain, even though she would not wish it upon anyone. She feared this unknown bloodlust, but she could not stop herself from enjoying it. As she whispered his name again, he whimpered as though it brought back a bad memory.

When she had explained her plan to Alan and Tuck, they knew she would not be stopped from seeing it through, but it made her feel more relaxed, knowing that she had backup if anything went wrong. Surprisingly, Alan and Tuck had agreed that it was a risk worth taking. Marian had seen how Gisbourne fought against his emotions, and some part of him did love her. She could use it to her advantage. It might not work, but it was worth a try.

Seeing Gisbourne weak and vulnerable in front of her, Marian considered how easy it would be to kill him, right here, right now. But she could never condone such actions as murdering a man in cold blood, at least not without a fair fight. She did not want to be like the Sheriff, and she refused to stoop to his level. She had to have some morals and boundaries not to cross. Marian quickly checked her exit route through the window was clear, and she eased into herself.

"You killed me Gisbourne, the one person you might have had a life with. You ruined your chance at a peaceful life, and now you are guilty. You will never be free of the burden."

#

Images swirled through Gisbourne's head, of death and destruction. Had he caused all this? He had never before cared about whose lives he ruined. But now that he had killed Marian, he did not know whether he could ever get over such a betrayal. Every night she haunted his dreams, turning once peaceful sleeps of

160

nothingness into torments of the mind and heart. She would certainly never have forgiven him for such a heinous, cowardly crime.

Before, he had always been able to justify the work the Sheriff offered him, but this was something else. He was dealing with the Sheriff's personal life for him and he did not like it. He thrived on seeking out outlaws and punishing them, but murdering innocents – especially the one person he loved – crossed the line. He was giving the Sheriff the revenge he wanted, without justifying it himself. He was the Sheriff's puppet and there was no escape for him now. He was destined for power and greatness, but always under another's authority. He would never be commander, but executioner. He was living a pointless existence.

Gisbourne sat up gasping and looked around. The chamber was still dark but he saw a shadow lingering and whipped his head around. He could not see her face, but he knew it was her. She would haunt him forever and there was no escape.

"Leave me alone," he ordered, as if it might help. She did not move, frozen in place.

"You have sinned, and you will never be forgiven for your crimes."

#

Suddenly Marian was holding a dagger to his throat, an instinct that drove her forward without thinking. Her face was just inches from his and she could see the whites of his eyes, the shock plain in his face. He sucked in a breath as the dagger scratched at his throat, releasing a ribbon of blood trailing down towards his chest. Marian watched as Gisbourne reached a hand to his neck, where the blood was running, and stared at the blood on his fingers in horror. Marian was certain he would realise that it really was her and kill her instantly, but instead he raised both hands in the air, surrendering.

"Kill me. Please kill me," he begged helplessly.

He really is a lost soul. Marian turned her back on him and climbed out of the window, not looking back.

#

"Marian, please tell us what happened," Alan repeated for what seemed like the millionth time. The sun was rising as they walked back to the barn, staying close to the shadows as always. Marian was getting better at it now, and her footsteps were barely heard on the squelchy forest floor.

"I had my chance. He was going to let me kill him, and I just left him." She could not believe that she had not killed Gisbourne when she had the chance. He had practically begged to die, and she found herself unable to commit the act. He deserved to suffer, and she would not give him the death he desired. She wanted him to be tormented by what he had done. *He is human, he does feel guilt.* He was not like the Sheriff after all. Now she knew Gisbourne's weakness, and he was only a threat to her while he lived under the Sheriff's command.

"Does he know you are alive?" Tuck asked.

She shrugged, unsure. "He might believe it was a bad dream, but I left a reminder. I do not know if he will tell the Sheriff or not. He seemed so... conflicted."

In front of her, Alan slowed and gestured for them to get down. Marian and Tuck crouched down to the ground as Alan crept closer to whatever he could sense. He had his sword in hand, ready to attack. Marian noticed his shoulders relax and he walked forward, putting his sword away. Marian stood and followed, curious.

More than twenty women stood in a cluster outside the barn. Marian was caught completely unawares. When they saw Alan, they all stepped away from him, concern growing in their expressions. Then they saw Marian. One woman stepped forward.

"Please, you have to help us. We have been trying to find you for ages."

#

It had taken Tobias quite some time to find Robin Hood. A scout had told him that Robin had moved on to a different part of the forest, although when he arrived at the location the scout had described, some of the gang had been there, but Robin's inner circle was nowhere to be seen. Nobody seemed to know where they had gone. All they knew was that they were on a special mission further north. They had no way of contacting Robin, which was very out of the ordinary.

Tobias had not been in Robin's gang for very long, but he knew Robin always left a messenger that knew how to find him, in case there was any trouble. Lately Robin had been acting strange, and he wondered if it was because of Marian. Rumours had spread through camp that they had a past, and she made something stir up inside Robin, some form of human emotions that he had locked away, out of reach.

Tobias had always yearned for love, but he had never found it. He was still young, only 16, but he knew that outlaws did not find love, in fact many had to leave their loved ones behind, which he thought would be a worse fate than never experiencing love. At least he did not know what he was missing.

He wanted to tell Robin of Marian's sacrifice to save him, to prove how strong and brave she really was. He had always known there was more to a woman than just providing a child, but Marian was incredible. He had never expected a woman of all people to save him, putting her own life in danger for a stranger. She was a far better person than any man and she had even inspired him to join their cause against corruption. Marian did not seem that confident about being in charge, but it was her instincts that led her forward, a natural leader that inspired loyalty. Although Robin did not inspire anything a great deal; he was kind enough to take in most outlaws but gave demands and did not care personally for any of them. That was probably why so many of his men had gone to Arthur.

Marian had something special that would lead men to fight in her honour. Robin needed to hear about this, and Tobias would not stop searching for him until he found him, no matter how long it would take. In camp, he collected supplies and headed north, weapons in hand, for he did not know what he might face.

#

Marian led the women into the barn to make sure they had not been followed or overheard. The women walked quietly, worried about something. Alan and Tuck stood guard at the door, mostly because the women felt uncomfortable around these men they did not know. The women did not speak at first.

"Please speak freely. How can I help you?"

"It is my husband. Guards came for him at night and took him away. They said if he resisted, he would be arrested. You have to help," one woman begged.

"Were your men taken too?" Marian asked the rest of the women.

"My son, he is only 12 years old, and my husband too."

"My father," said another woman.

They all started shouting to get Marian's attention. This was the wrong way to deal with such a situation. Marian stood on a rotting hay bale overlooking them.

"You say your men were taken. Did any of the guards suggest where they may be going?" They silenced as she spoke.

One woman stepped forward. "I heard them talking outside my home. They said they needed all the men they could get to join them. They were going to kill an outlaw who was hiding in the forest. I do not think they mean you, they said they were going north."

"Do not worry. I will find a way to get your men back safe, especially those too old or young to fight. I give you my word. You must continue with your daily lives, make it seem like nothing has changed. We do not want to raise suspicion."

"Marian?" She recognised the voice instantly and looked to the doorway.

"Alice. What are you doing here?" Marian started towards her, worried about what news she may bring. One of the women blocked her path.

"Marian? The recluse?"

"Yes," Marian replied hesitantly, uneasy that her identity was no longer a secret. Now it would not be long before news spread.

"Marian, our hero!" the woman cheered. Marian had half expected her to be a spy of the Sheriff's, but she was becoming too paranoid for her own good.

"I am no hero," she said honestly. These women did not just hope she would save their men but believed she could not fail. The pressure was too much for her. She had no idea where the men were, let alone how to rescue them. She was vastly outnumbered.

"But you are," Alice spoke out. "Marian is the hero we have all been waiting for. She will bring us hope and take away our fear." Murmurs of agreement echoed around the barn.

Marian addressed the women, trying to stop the praise she did not deserve. "Gisbourne and the Sheriff attempted to get rid of me, but they cannot know I am alive. They believe I am dead and, for everyone's safety, it needs to stay that way. I will do what I can to find out what has happened. Return home and carry on as normal."

The women all nodded in agreement and slowly they left, a few at a time, so as not to attract attention. Tuck showed them the route back, while Alan remained on guard at the door. Alice walked over to Marian.

"I want to help. I have been training and I want to learn from you. Please let me."

"First of all, Alice, I need you as a contact for the people of Nottingham. Please help them and let me know of any problems. I know I have neglected my promise to you. You are strong, stronger than me, but in different ways. I trust that you can do this, and you know how to find me. I cannot be in two places at once, especially now that I need to try to keep up the ruse of my death a little longer. I cannot venture far into Nottingham at the moment." She could sense Alice's disappointment, but she did not speak out against it. She nodded and left without a word. Marian promised herself to give some time to Alice soon, but she had too much to sort out first. She just could not bring herself to put Alice in danger's way, not yet anyway.

"I am guessing you have a plan?" Alan asked.

"Half a plan at least. First, we find the guards, hopefully still preparing the men for travel. If they are to be extra man power, then they must be given weapons to seem strong enough to pose a threat to whoever the Sheriff is going after. Trust me, if the Sheriff is taking precautions in this mission of his, then we should be prepared for anything. We will follow them and find out what is happening before we decide what our plan of action is. We need to be careful."

"I am presuming you will not be trying to talk Tuck and I out of coming with you?"

"I need all the man power I can get, even if that is just the three of us. I wish the people would take a stand. They are putting all their hopes on me, instead of trying to do something themselves."

"Perhaps this is their test," Tuck replied, cryptically. Marian wondered if he did get an insight into the future, from God or some other force. Or perhaps he simply just saw things differently. She never understood what he meant, until it unfolded in front of her.

She was pleased to have such good company. Without Alan and Tuck, she would never have become the strong, powerful woman she felt like now. She worried how long it would last until something went wrong. Somehow, she always ended up making things worse rather than better.

Chapter 27

Marian, Tuck and Alan followed the Sheriff's entourage as they were led deeper into the forest. There were at least a hundred men, some mere boys and others too old; who could barely walk, let alone fight. The townspeople wore their own clothes; they had not been given anything to protect themselves with, other than a weapon. Most did not even know how to hold a sword, dangling it uselessly in their hands. It was sickening to see such ill-treated people being forced to help a Sheriff who did not care about their lives, who saw them as nothing more than rodents, when the Sheriff was the real pest. Marian struggled to look over the top of the men to see what was happening. The Sheriff was sheltered in a grand carriage surrounded by his real guards, with full suits of armour and the best of the weapons.

"I have to get close to the carriage. I might be able to find out more of what they are planning," she whispered to Alan.

"It is best I stay at the back to keep watch on the situation. I will only slow you down. Both of you find a way to get nearer the front," Tuck added.

Alan nodded his agreement and Marian led him slowly through the people. Marian sympathised for these people, forced into war, to fight on the wrong side. The older men were already starting to slow, getting caught up at the back, but Marian suspected Tuck would find some encouragement to keep them going.

She ploughed forward. Some turned to her questioningly and she could feel their hope, like a fire burning brighter as it spread. Guilt consumed her unexpectedly. They were accepting that she would save them. What if she could not protect them from what might come?

She did not understand what was going on herself, how could she inspire the people to blindly follow her?

The men started to whisper among themselves, spreading the word. Marian's nerves were on edge.

"Keep quiet. They cannot know we are here," Alan whispered to those surrounding them. Immediately, the swell of men closed tighter around them. She prayed, not to God, but to herself, for a way to save them all.

#

Tobias was lost in limbo. His mind was full of doubt and he could do nothing to stop it from eating away at him. He had rested in a small cave overnight and started off again at sunrise. It was at least midday by now, with the sun at its peak. It was a hot day, he trudged on, trying to stay positive. He could not give up now that he had come this far. He did not understand why he thought it so important to deliver such an insignificant message, and very out of date by the time he would find Robin. He slowed as he heard movement nearby. There were voices in the distance and Tobias hung close to the trees. As he crept closer, he recognised Robin's voice. He felt a surge of relief. He was just about to step out into the open when he heard another voice. Arthur a Bland, the rogue outlaw. His blood ran cold.

This man had torn the gang apart. Tobias was not angry, as Robin should have seen it coming all along. Robin was not exactly the greatest leader and he had neglected his men to the extent that many had been easily persuaded by Arthur. Of course, Tobias had no idea about it until Robin had sent him and every single other outlaw he could find, to reveal Arthur's deception, and give him no choice but to surrender. It had worked, but Tobias had seen the betrayal hit Robin, stabbed in the back by someone he had trusted. It had made him even less present than he already had been. He would now leave for days without explanation, only to return like nothing had happened.

Tobias had not expected Robin to meet Arthur again. This must be why he had been so secretive about this mission. Tobias listened to the conversation, using it as an opportunity to find out why Robin was talking with him and not killing him, as he had promised to do. He could not make sense of it.

"You asked me here, so I came. I have been following you around for a day and you still have not told me why you need me here. I could have killed you. You told me your location and myself or my loyal men could have killed you on the spot, just as I promised. But I gave you my word and now I think you have betrayed me once again. This is a wild goose chase. What are you waiting for?"

"I want a truce. I am sorry for the betrayal, but I am a changed man. I am in your debt. I want to show you something for my gratitude, if only you will follow and trust me."

Tobias noticed Little John up ahead, and Will behind them. If Robin was not worried about Arthur, he would not have brought his two best men.

They continued forward, walking strangely parallel to Nottingham and Tobias wondered where they were going, whether it was a coincidence. Tobias did not in any way trust Arthur so he decided to stay hidden and follow, just in case they needed him, and he admitted to himself, he was curious. He had never been a good outlaw, and this could get him into trouble, but he could not help himself.

#

Before Marian could get close enough to the Sheriff's carriage, Alan pulled her backwards into the thicker part of the crowd. She stumbled, losing her balance. She whirled around to him and was about to protest, but his expression was serious. She followed his gaze to the front of the entourage. They were turning, not just going in a different direction, but also slowing down until they were in a complete circle, surrounding a small area in the middle. Marian tried to wriggle her way to the front of the group to see, but she had to be slow to avoid any attention on her. She looked to her right, where the carriage opened and Gisbourne stepped out. Behind him, the Sheriff appeared. She heard the screech of weapons being drawn. The people looked around at one another and slowly they prepared their weapons the best they could, the fear of what they would face forcing them to ready themselves. It echoed around the circle like a ripple effect as they all followed suit. Marian still could not see anything. She pushed her way forward as far as she dared without being out in the open, and then she saw them.

#

Robin looked around frantically for an escape route, but there was nowhere to run; they were completely surrounded. He took a deep breath, trying to keep his head clear. His men were relying on him. Even though Will, Little John and himself were the best fighters of his gang, they could not even hope to defeat so many soldiers. They were surrounded at every angle and there was no way they would escape. He was trapped like an animal, hunted down and facing death.

Arthur did not look surprised at all. It was then that he realised he had fallen for it again. He really had lost his mind. Out of everything, he did not expect this sort of betrayal. Arthur was obviously working with his enemy, Gisbourne, to get rid of him. Arthur knew many of Robin's secrets, like the time he stole directly from Prince John, a few years ago. He could use it all against him, and he had done so, to save himself. Robin laughed inwardly at his idiocy.

This is what he had always told his men to do. It was every man for himself; and now, only now, Robin realised how wrong he had been. His father had been right; he was no leader.

Two men approached him, one he recognised as Gisbourne and the one behind must be the High Sheriff, dressed in his finest attire. Selfishly, thinking of Nottingham brought up a longing for Marian he had hoped had disappeared by now.

Arthur stepped forward, towards Gisbourne who put up a hand to stop him.

"You have done well Arthur. You have kept your side of the bargain and so I will keep mine. You are free," Gisbourne announced begrudgingly.

"Wait." The Sheriff stepped forward. Gisbourne looked at him, surprise flickering across his carefully blank, tired-looking face. "I made no such promise. An outlaw is an outlaw." He looked around at his men. "Attack the outlaws, kill them. They deserve no better than slaughter."

#

Tobias watched in horror as Robin, Will and Little John readied their weapons for their final fight. Without thinking, his legs took him forward from the outside of the circle, through the soldiers, who amazingly let him through without a fight. He did not know what he would do when he got there, but he needed to help. Marian had taught him that every life is worth saving, but not everyone would survive this.

Somehow, he reached the centre, close to the Sheriff. He was unsure whether this was a good thing or not. The armoured guards in the clearing were so focused on the outlaws in the centre that they had not thought of someone coming in from the outside and that the Sheriff may need protecting from every angle. He noticed Robin struggling to keep the guards off and ran at the Sheriff at full speed. Tobias pulled him backwards and put his sword to his neck. The Sheriff shrieked in horror and Gisbourne turned. Gisbourne froze for a moment, appearing to consider whether the Sheriff was worth saving. The Sheriff hissed his name and Gisbourne advanced.

"Stop the guards or I slit his throat." Tobias had never been confident but somehow his voice came out powerful and clear.

"Do it," the Sheriff whispered hoarsely. Tobias's heart was pumping both fear and exhilaration through his body, spurring him on.

"STOP!" Gisbourne boomed, and Tobias relaxed a little. He had solely managed to stop the fighting.

Before he could rejoice or even realise his mistake, something whirled through the air towards him. Tobias was pushed off his feet, pain stabbing through his shoulder. He fell in a heap on the floor, gripping his injured arm. The Sheriff stood a few feet away from him, looking down with a wicked smile. As he started towards Tobias, Gisbourne whispered something to the Sheriff and he whirled around on his heels, forgetting about him.

#

Marian was aware only of Robin Hood in the centre, fighting stronger than she would expect, but even he could only hold them off for so long. She was torn. She did not want to be found out by the Sheriff, but she could not let these men die. The men around her moved forward slowly, none wanting to engage with the fight. She heard Gisbourne shout and suddenly the chaos turned to deathly silence. Marian noticed Tobias holding a sword to the Sheriff's neck and she smiled. She did not know how he had gotten there, but she respected him for it. Relief flooded through her at the sight of the Sheriff looking so vulnerable. Tuck appeared beside them.

"This is not going to last long, Marian. You need to talk to your people. You cannot win by yourself."

Marian was not ready, but she had little choice. She took a deep breath and felt the crowd shuffle away, leaving a circle around her. She was now the centre of attention, and her ruse was about to be revealed to the world. While the attention of the guards and the Sheriff were at the other end, this was her chance. She tried to push the thought of Robin to the back of her mind and focused on what she could do to help.

"I know I am not a hero. I have done many things I regret. I make mistakes and I am in no way perfect. But I am human, and I fight for what is right. Killing anyone, innocent or otherwise, is wrong. I stand for justice. Justice against the corrupt and the cruel; against the Sheriff of Nottingham, who would do anything for power. I will not be disappointed if you do not wish to fight, but I ask you this. Are you going to be ruled by fear your whole lives, or are you going to stand up against it?"

Silence.

"I promise you this. No matter how long it takes, I will seek justice for the people. You are not slaves, you should not be treated as such. You are people and you deserve to be free. You should be free to earn money and keep it. Fear inspires fear, not loyalty. Do not take the easy road to your self-destruction, stand up and fight. Who will stand and fight with me?" The silence lasted a little longer and suddenly battle cries swept through the crowds around Marian.

"Those unable to fight and those who do not wish to fight; Tuck will take you back to safety. The rest of you, ready your weapons. We fight."

Marian waited as around half the men followed Tuck away from the fighting. Marian took the moment to assess the situation around her. She heard the Sheriff and Gisbourne calling everyone to fight once more, and she worried for Tobias. The Sheriff had managed to get away from him and she knew they would not let him live. Her eyes locked on Robin and he was looking directly back at her, his eyes wide. She felt her heart flutter at the sight of him but she pushed it down. She could not have any distractions right now. She ripped her gaze away from him, and noticed a surge of guards coming towards her, with Gisbourne and the Sheriff in the centre.

#

Robin kept his sights on Marian, fearing for her life. As she had turned, noticing the guards storming through the people, he too had seen it. He could not control his heart the way he used to be able to.

"Will, John, get Tobias to safety."

"No, we are coming with you," Little John announced. Robin knew there was never any way to stop Little John doing what he wanted. "For Marian."

"For Marian," Will agreed, for once no sarcastic comments to make. Robin could not understand their loyalty to Marian, perhaps it was similar to the way he felt towards her.

The Sheriff had forgotten about them and had all his guards' attention on Marian.

They followed the guards towards her.

#

Fear gripped Marian, not for herself but for the people who were willing to fight with her. She had acted strong to them, as there was no other way, but she was terrified. They were not equipped to fight armoured, trained guards. She could not let them fight to their deaths.

"Stay back. This is personal. Make way for the guards to get through."

Alan was a little way away from Marian and he looked at her worriedly. Marian shook her head and focused on the situation. Gisbourne and the Sheriff knew she was alive. She did not want to hide behind her people. She could not let others die protecting her. The guards closed a circle around her, with both the Sheriff and Gisbourne inside.

"I told you she was still alive," Gisbourne gloated. The Sheriff did not acknowledge him.

"Guards, turn your backs. Make sure no one interrupts," the Sheriff ordered. "Well, Marian, you really are a master of disguise. You set that filthy outlaw free, and he almost killed me. Shame, he would have made a great soldier. He is bleeding to death somewhere over there."

"At least you admit you are not invincible."

"I speak the truth, you know I always do." The Sheriff looked around the crowd. "You know they are not just your people. I disguised some of my own men, in case anyone tried to stand up against me. Look now, you will see."

Marian saw that some of the men were moving to the outside of the group, their swords drawn on the townspeople. Her plan was falling apart, the Sheriff had won again. She would never beat him. Her fate was left to him once more.

"What do you want?" She was struggling for breath. Her uncle would never leave her, never let her be.

"I want you to come quietly. If you do, you have my word that they will be free to return to Nottingham and carry on their worthless existence. If you refuse,

I will kill them all, including the outlaws you are trying to protect. The choice is yours."

"It is no choice."

"There is always a choice. I know you will choose differently than I."

"Because you are reckless and uncaring; you would always let others die before you. I will die before I let you harm anyone."

"How noble. Speaking of which, please stop your lover from trying to save you."

For a moment, Marian did not understand what he meant. Then she noticed he was looking at Robin. She spun around seeing him advance on the guards.

Marian looked to Alan, hopelessly. She knew he would not want her to sacrifice herself, but there was no way to stop her, and he would understand. "Every man for himself," Marian whispered, and she diverted her attention to Robin and back.

#

Alan knew what Marian was going to do. He did not like it at all, but perhaps she had no choice in the matter. He would respect her wishes no matter what. He had once told her that an outlaw's motto was 'every man for himself' and that is what Marian wanted right now. Even though she was sacrificing herself, she wanted everyone else to be free. He ran towards Robin and stopped him just before he reached the guards.

"What are you doing? We need to get Marian out!" Robin yelled hysterically at Alan.

"Marian is doing this for us, for everyone. We need to get out of here. I think she is sacrificing herself for everyone else to live. We will not give up, but we need to let this happen then come up with a plan. I do not think they would kill her here, with so many angry people. We will have time to come up with something. Trust me, please, Robin."

Chapter 28

Marian lay on the cold, damp floor of the gaol cell, staring at the ceiling. She had been pushed into the smallest, foulest smelling cell but she did not care. She guessed she had been there a couple of hours, though there was no light down here, making it almost impossible to tell the passing of time.

It had not been a long journey back. She had been wedged into the Sheriff's carriage between two broad guards, opposite Gisbourne and her uncle. Gisbourne had looked pale, and she avoided his gaze the entire journey as he watched her. It was uncomfortable, to say the least, but far worse lay ahead for her. The Sheriff had ordered the driver to go as fast as he could, leaving behind the outlaws, people and even the Sheriff's own guards. Marian was his priority, and he was keeping to his promise. This was still personal to him, but he would make a spectacle of her. He now knew that she was leading a revolution against him and he would stop the threat as quick as possible, meaning Marian would be dead soon.

She was not afraid. She felt a calm wash upon her like a wave of warmth, shielding her from the nothingness of the cell. She knew what lay ahead for her and her fate was sealed. There was no escape this time. She hoped the Sheriff's guards had kept the bargain and not assassinated the outlaws or the people. Marian could not help but wonder if it would have been better to let Robin die. Things would have turned out differently. For one, the Sheriff and Gisbourne would still believe Marian to be dead, but also, she would not have gotten the poor innocents of Nottingham caught up in the situation. The Sheriff was angry and there was nothing she could do in here, locked away.

There was movement close by and footsteps approached her cell. Marian sat up, squinting to see through the shadows. Her cell door opened with a screech that set her teeth on edge and it banged shut, the metallic noise echoing in her ears. Marian looked up and stared into Gisbourne's lost eyes.

"I am sorry, but this is the way it has to be. I need to prove my loyalty to the Sheriff." Two guards appeared, turning Marian around and holding her against the floor. She heard a familiar noise, air rushing and an excruciating pain tore through her back, igniting a million tiny fires of agony.

#

As soon as the carriage holding Gisbourne, the Sheriff and Marian had left, chaos had once again erupted. As soon as the carriage was out of sight, the guards prepared to attack, and the traitor Arthur had run from his hiding spot behind a tree before Robin could stop him. Alan had noticed some of the guards looking uncertainly for a leader to tell them what to do, but others advanced on the outlaws. It had been a surreal experience, and the outlaws had been ready to fight if they had to, but the strangest thing happened.

The people stepped in, blocking the guards' route to the outlaws. It was an amazing sight; the people coming together, standing their ground to create a wall between the guards and the outlaws. For the first time, the people were standing up for what was right. He had watched Robin's face change from confusion to shock and then to the realisation of what this meant. The people were willing to risk their lives to save others, just as Marian had asked of them. The guards had paused for a few moments, unsure how to react, but Alan could clearly see by the lowering of their weapons, that they did not want to fight innocent people who would not fight back. They had promptly left in a wave of exhaustion, marching back to Nottingham.

Now there was peace, and it was starting to get dark, but Robin was still pacing, clearly at war with his emotions. Alan watched him impatiently, waiting for a response. Robin looked a little worse for wear, but to be honest, they all did. Whatever Marian had been promised; they had not kept their word.

Tobias was injured, with an arrow piercing his shoulder. Robin had pulled it out, with a whimper from Tobias. Alan had been surprised by Tobias's bravery at holding a sword to the Sheriff's throat and had a renewed sense of admiration for him.

Tuck was now escorting the people back to Nottingham while Alan waited to find out what Robin was going to do. He wanted to run straight to Marian and get her out, but he would only get caught and that would in no way help Marian. He stayed with Robin, hoping he would help.

"I cannot believe Robin would give up everything for Marian! I know she is a lady and Robin has mushy feelings for her, but I did not think he would act on it!" Alan, as usual, fought the urge to knock some sense into Will.

"Alan, you did not hear Robin. He was like a man possessed. I am glad he finally let his emotions out." Little John rarely spoke so many words.

"I had to let Marian do what she had to do. If I had let Robin step in..." She would have hated Alan forever. He could not finish the sentence. They may not have lived to get that far, but he would be lost to the world anyway if she blamed him.

Little John and Will stood with Alan in silence. An unspoken brotherhood.

#

Robin could not stop thinking about Marian and the sacrifice she had made to save not just him, but everyone. Why would someone put another person's life before their own? He could not understand it. Surely it was more important to save yourself than to give up just for the sake of others? Or was it? Was this what Robin had lost so long ago? He looked at Will and Little John, who would do almost anything for him. Would they sacrifice themselves to save him? He knew Alan would. It was only right that Robin should save Marian. He owed her for she had saved his life and many others.

"John, Will, find a physician for Tobias."

"No. We should all help Marian," Will said matter-of-fact, very out of character.

"But that goes against our rules," Robin replied almost automatically.

"*Your* rules, Robin. Change is coming," Little John corrected.

He could not stop them from helping. Taking this risk felt right, but it went against everything he had ever believed in.

"Are you sure Robin?" Alan asked. Robin ignored him.

"Tobias, can you walk? We leave now while there is still light."

#

Quiet fell among the people as they neared Nottingham. Tuck suspected it was a mark of respect to Marian for saving them. She would be made an example of, to make the people bow down to the Sheriff's authority. Although Tuck knew it could have the opposite effect, maybe even turn her into a saint or martyr, which in his eyes she already was. Tuck believed that the people would do what was right, although most important to them first was to be reunited with their families, so that Marian's sacrifice would not be wasted.

Tuck stopped as they reached the border of the forest into Nottingham. He turned to the people.

"God has a purpose for you all. Remember that you have been spared this night for a reason, and Marian has sacrificed her life for you."

Tuck was starting to believe this was God's plan all along. If he had not lost his faith in the first place, this would not have been the outcome. Marian had helped the people stand up against the corrupt. He looked up into the sky, where somewhere Heaven was waiting and God was watching him. He could feel the presence wash over him. He walked away from the people and went to his old church.

The church was silent and empty. The people were at home spending time with their families now that they were safe. Tuck knelt down at the front. It was a glorious place, and he could feel the energy buzzing around him. He looked into the eyes of Jesus on the cross.

"I have questioned your choices. I lost belief in you. I forgot my purpose. You have given me everything and I have earned none of it. I see it now. It is all coming together, and I can feel you. You are with me and I will continue to follow your guidance, and reach out to the people, as your plan for me declared. I will fight for Nottingham, in every way possible, and I will not stop until my last breath. Thank you, God, for making me see the truth."

#

Marian tried to be strong, but she could not help but hide herself as best she could. She attempted to sit up, but pain rippled through her. She gave up and lay on her side, shivering from pain and the cold. Fresh blood spattered the walls a dark crimson. There were others in the gaol, but she did not want anyone to see her like this, so instead she tried to stay silent. She hugged herself tightly, to keep in any warmth. Her cloak was torn, and her arms were bare. She could feel the blood trickling down her back, the only warming sensation. If only she still had a weapon, she could play the coward and end her life here. She longed for death at this moment. It could not get any worse than this.

Murmurs came from the other cells and Marian raised her head to see a shadow throwing scraps of food to each prisoner. When the person came closer to Marian's cell, she could see it was a young woman.

"Please, come over here," the woman whispered. Marian crawled painfully over to the cell door. "My name is Emma, I am Beatrice's friend. I have been keeping an eye on the castle for her. I am sorry I cannot help you. I just want to thank you for being you. You are what the people need." She sucked in a breath as she saw the blood. "Here, the Sheriff told me to give you this to wear tomorrow." Marian could not see her face, but she could hear the sniffling; Emma was crying.

"What is wrong? Is it your son, George?"

"How do you know about him?"

"I saw you once, after your husband died. I asked Beatrice to become your friend and help you any way she could. Is George getting worse?"

"He is dead." Emma broke down, rushing away.

Now it definitely could not get any worse than this. George, an innocent boy, lost too soon. Emma was alone like too many others.

Marian must have slept for a few hours for she was awoken by the rattling of a key. She sat up too quickly, remembering her fresh wounds, but forced herself to stay upright. For a moment, she hoped it might be someone to rescue her, but then she saw three guards and realised once more that she would not be saved, not this time. Without a word, they dragged her up onto her feet, past the rest of the gaol cells, and into the torture chamber. When Walter had been alive, he had never put anyone into this hellish room.

The room stunk of rotting blood and the walls were stained with it too, the remnants of recent tortures. Marian shivered at the disturbing sight of it. She felt a shove and suddenly she was lying face down on the stained floor, her face scratching on stone. One of the guards pulled her by the hair, forcing her to look up. The Sheriff sat in front of her smiling his usual wicked grin of victory.

"We cannot have you looking like a saint now, can we? I want the people to fear me, more than ever. I want them to see you are weak." A foot swung towards her and connected with her cheek. Tasting blood in her mouth, she spat at her uncle's shoe, her last victory. She was not afraid of him anymore.

#

Daylight was here and, as expected, news spread of a public execution. Robin, Alan, Tuck, Will and Little John all stood in the shadows, watching the guards as they pulled people from their homes, forcing them towards the castle courtyard. They had known the Sheriff would want everyone there, as a deterrent from revolution. Alan did not understand Little John and Will's desire to help Marian, but they were kind, for outlaws, and they were the only family he had.

Tobias had wanted to help, but he was wounded and recovering. None of them were healers, but Alan had watched Marian's physician and knew the basics, so they had left Tobias with wet cloth to keep his wound clean and bandages for him to replace. He was well enough to take care of himself and they could not afford to lose any others to look after him. They left him in the barn to keep him away from the danger.

Robin had not told them of any plan to save Marian, and Alan thought it similar to the way Marian ran into situations and thought on the spot. He hated not having a plan to follow but they did not know what to expect today. The Sheriff was capable of anything.

For once, Will was silent. Apart from Alan, none of the outlaws had set foot in a town or village in years, they must be nervous. Alan was not nervous; he only worried about Marian. The Sheriff could have already killed her for all he knew. They may be too late.

Robin had been right about one thing; Alan had never seen so many guards placed around the castle before. Many of the people who had been at the scene last night were in the crowds, looking worn out but holding their wives and daughters protectively. A couple of them held eye contact with Alan and quickly closed around the outlaws, hiding them in the crowds as they entered the courtyard. Alan gave a nod to some of those around him as a gesture of gratitude. Apart from Tuck who was speaking in a hushed tone, Alan guessed perhaps a prayer to God, none of the others seemed to care at all about the people around them. Everyone from the entire town, and perhaps further afield, seemed to be there and that was exactly what the Sheriff wanted. Alan felt like cattle being herded.

A loud bang rippled across the courtyard. Alan turned to see that the gates had closed, with even more people outside of them looking into the courtyard. There was no way out. He wondered if perhaps this was a slaughter, but the Sheriff did need the people, he could not simply kill everyone in Nottingham. To be powerful and rich, and to stay in Prince John's inner circle, he needed the people. Alan longed for the day King Richard would return to England and start fighting against the corrupt in England rather than fighting insignificant battles abroad.

"Spread out," Robin whispered, and they dispersed among the crowd.

#

Alice was afraid, more so than she had ever been in her life. She was terrified that Marian would die and she would be unable to do anything about it. She understood why Marian did not want Alice to put herself in danger, but it hurt all the same. She was ready to prove herself and she was tired of abiding by the rules and to the Sheriff's authority.

In the early hours of the morning, guards had banged on the manor's door. Alice and Beatrice had hurried to see if it was Marian, but the guards only brought news of a public execution. Her stomach roiled, knowing Marian was going to hang today. Now they stood beside one another, staring at the horror that was the gallows. Neither of them had ever been to an execution, they had managed to avoid it until now. But this was Marian.

Alice noticed a familiar face; Alan made his way past her and she grabbed his arm.

"What are you doing here?" Alice asked. "Are you going to save Marian?"

"Keep out of this Alice, for your own good." He tried to get away from her, but her grip was firm.

"No. You cannot do it alone. I want to help."

"Alice…" Beatrice protested. "They will be fine. He already has help."

"So, we are just going to carry on like nothing happened, follow the rules like always. I cannot do it any longer." She turned back to Alan. "Please, I have to do this."

There was no changing Alice's mind. If he did not let her, she would follow him anyway. "Alright, but stay close and try not to attract any attention to us."

Beatrice huffed. "I guess I will play babysitter today. I cannot have either of you run into any trouble, not without me."

The great doors opened and out trickled various nobles from around Nottingham and even further reaching areas. This was a grand display to the Sheriff, of his power and influence. The nobles took seats at the top of the stairs, then Gisbourne walked out, standing half way down the steps, scanning the crowd. Several guards marched out, and in the middle of them was the Sheriff of Nottingham.

"My people. I am here today to set the record straight. I believe you have been misled and I forgive you for your sins against me. You are always welcome under my rule. I am but your humble servant. I ensure your money is put to good use and it goes back into the economy, although your delicate brains may not understand such politics. I promise, though it may be tough right now, that we will benefit as a town of great standing. We will be Prince John's seat of power, and he will bring greatness to this fertile land. Trust me; I was put in this position to serve you.

"Now, down to business. This girl promised you things that were not hers to give. She is but a girl who does not understand politics or authority. Her ideas should be ridiculed. She misled you. You will now see her in her true form. Death will be a release for such a devil." The Sheriff was a very theatrical person and this event was his biggest spectacle to date. Alice half expected there to be drums involved to add to the tension but instead there was only a deafening silence. She would have preferred drums to mute her heart that felt as though it were about to leap out of her chest.

Slowly a small group of guards appeared from the castle. Alice wondered why they were going so slowly until she spotted Marian, in a bloodstained dress that used to be white, struggling to put one foot in front of another. Her heart contracted and the world around her collapsed.

Chapter 29

As Marian approached her execution, she tried to remain calm, but nothing would still her churning stomach and shaking hands. She knew she must look just as the Sheriff had intended her to be; weak and powerless. Her body was a throbbing mess of bruises, broken bones and blood. She did not even understand how she was still putting one foot in front of the other. She struggled to keep herself together.

She reached the gallows and was pushed down to her knees. It was a hard push, but with her frailty at this moment, even a slight breeze could knock her down. Her knees struck wood with a painful thud.

Gisbourne readied a bow and arrow. Marian had never seen Gisbourne with a bow before, she suspected it was not his weapon of choice, but of course the Sheriff would want her to be killed the most personal way possible. Gisbourne looked at war with himself as he pointed the arrow towards Marian, and she closed her eyes ready for impact.

#

Alice took one glance at Alan and Beatrice, then ran forward. They were going to do nothing to help Marian, she could not let this happen. She stopped as she came to the front of the crowd. She heard Alan shout behind her but blocked him out.

"Gisbourne, you know Marian is a good person! She does not deserve this. Look at her. Do you not think she has suffered enough?" She did not know if it would work, but she had to try. He liked Marian, in his own sadistic way, and she attempted to play on it.

Alice looked back at Alan. He was doing nothing to help the situation. She searched the crowd and found another face she recognised, Robin Hood. He was not looking at Marian, but at Gisbourne instead. Alice turned her attention back to Gisbourne, who was hesitating. Alice had managed to distract him. Gisbourne still held a spark for Marian, after all. Gasps went through the crowds as Gisbourne whirled around and the arrow whistled through the air, striking the Sheriff, in the centre of his chest, where his heart would have been, if he had one.

#

Marian heard gasps from the crowds and she opened her eyes, looking down at herself. She stared in disbelief as she realised she was still alive, no more wounded than she had been before. She gazed around, trying to make sense of it. Gisbourne had his back to her. Marian peered around him and saw the Sheriff unconscious on the floor, the arrow meant for her piercing his chest. He was dead. There were no tricks now, he really was dead. Marian let out a sigh of relief, a weight lifting off her. She regretted it instantly as her vision blurred and she fell to the floor, puffing with exhaustion.

Noise erupted around the courtyard. The guards looked around, confused. The two guards closest to Marian were pulled backwards as the people dragged them away from her, coming together in groups, beating the guards. A guard started towards her, but she had no energy to move. Unexpectedly someone sprung in between her and her attacker. Robin! He plunged his sword into the guard before he could even scream and dropped to the ground without a sound.

Robin would always be her hero, her saviour. He pulled her up towards him and she let him, unable to hold herself up. He let her put her weight on him and Alan had reached her other side, having fought his way through the crowd. He was sweating but unharmed, to her relief. Then Alice and Beatrice appeared, panting. Alice carried a dagger, and Marian could tell Alice was ready now. If Alice wanted to fight, then she would prefer it to be with her so that she could look out for her.

Robin whistled and both Little John and Will appeared from the chaos. Little John stood ahead of them, pushing people out of the way with his staff, and thumping any guards that got in their way, clearing a path towards the gate. She heard Tuck grunt in protest and Marian followed his line of sight, seeing, with regret, that the gate was shut. Past the gate, there was more chaos; people fleeing with their families, and outlaws fighting more guards in an attempt to reach the gate.

"The gate opens at the top, up there," Marian pointed to above the gate.

"Wait here," Will yelled and before anyone could stop him, he was already climbing the steps, fighting off guards as he made his way towards the contraption. Robin shot arrows ahead of Will, stopping guards in their tracks, though he was not fast enough to stop them all.

Will faced a few guards but quickly stopped them.

#

Will had sight of his target, a winding mechanism above the gate. He ran as fast as his legs could take him, not looking back. This was his moment to shine, to be the hero. He started to raise the gate and dozens of people started running towards it. Will heard Robin shout a warning but he carried on, determined.

He thought of his wife who had been told he was dead. She would never know the truth and he regretted that he would never see her face again. He loved her and when he had been forced to leave, she had just told him she was expecting a child. He did not know whether his child was a boy or girl but only that they would be five years old by now. He prayed they were healthy. Will had always been the joker of the gang, but deep down he was hiding behind it, trying to bury his past life. He apologised inwardly for not visiting his family, for being cruel and stealing mercilessly. He had turned into someone he no longer recognised and hated himself for it. This was his redemption, his last confession.

He pulled the ropes until the gate would rise no more and felt a burst of pain ripple through him. *If there is a heaven, take me there.*

#

Marian sucked in a breath as she watched the sword pierce through Will's back. Alan threw his knife, and it knocked the guard, but it was too late; Will was dead. Alan pulled Marian to lean on him and he thumped Robin in the back to keep him moving. The gate closed just as they crossed it. The majority of people had managed to get out; only the few who were beating helpless guards remained. Marian focused on what lay ahead and tried to forget the past. This was a new beginning.

At least thirty of Robin's gang had shown up to help at the castle and now they were running behind Robin. Alan slowed, Marian weakening her grip on him.

"Robin, we need to get her to a physician. There is one Marian trusts not far from here."

Robin nodded, "Lead the way." He turned to his followers. Marian noticed that a few of the townspeople were among his men too. "Those of you who helped us, please return to your homes. My men, return to the forest. Stay nearby; I must speak with you tomorrow. Set up camp and I will find you."

#

Robin stood guard outside the physician's for most of the night. He could not bear to see Marian in pain and he had been thrown out by Alan just as he caught a glimpse of what looked like scars and fresh whip marks on her back. He had been so selfish with her, even losing one of his own men to rescue her. *Poor Will*, Robin thought. He knew nothing about his life; in fact, he knew nothing about any of his men, even those he was closest to. He had ignored them so often and expected everything from them. There was no reason for them to be loyal to him after he had treated them like soldiers for so long.

Robin could not be here, in England anymore. He needed to get away, take his mind off everything and work out who he really was. He felt more lost than ever before. He did not understand his feelings towards Marian and it was getting him into trouble. He was exhausted of living like this, pretending he did not care about anything. He had forgotten what it was like to feel anything at all. He could not leave Marian again without an explanation though.

He would have to wait until he was allowed back in to speak to her, just one last time.

#

The person Marian saw first when she awoke was Robert, her physician. She was in his home, and Beatrice was there too. As soon as Beatrice noticed she was awake, she rushed over.

"Marian, always getting yourself into these silly situations. What were you thinking? Walter would never have consented to you putting yourself in such danger. And Alice, the stupid girl. You are too alike."

"I want to see Robin," was all she could reply.

Alan was beside Beatrice. "Shall I get him for you? He is just outside."

"I am so sorry about Will." Her eyes filled with tears. He had died for her, and nobody had expected it. She had not even really gotten to know him, and yet he had risked everything to save her.

"It was none of our faults. He made his choice. None of us could have stopped him. Many put their lives in danger last night," he tried to console her.

"I know and all for me. None of you should have been there." Again, she was to blame. Her list of regrets was growing too long.

"You should not doubt yourself, you have brought the people together. You should have seen them when you made that deal with the Sheriff. When you left with him, the guards turned on us. But the townspeople, they formed a barrier and the guards could not bring themselves to attack those who would not fight back. It was an incredible sight and all because of you. The Sheriff is dead. He can never hurt you again."

"Where is everyone?" Marian sat up, feeling dizzy but forced herself to stay upright.

She had a new nightdress on; Beatrice must have bought it for her.

"Robin sent the outlaws back to the forest. They are holding a ceremony to commemorate Will. It was Little John's idea. We used to simply forget the past, but we realise now that everyone is important, and every sacrifice should be remembered."

"That is a lovely idea," Marian agreed.

"Right, I will get Robin." He turned to Beatrice and Robert. "Give them some privacy."

Alan and Robert left, but Beatrice paused at the door.

"Where is Alice?" Marian asked.

"She is fine. I left her sleeping. She has been training hard, turning into a little warrior. She reminds me of someone." She nodded at Marian and left.

"Marian?" Robin tapped at the door and entered.

"Robin. I need to thank you for last night. You and your men should not have risked all that just for me."

"We all came of our own free will. I did not force any of them to join me. They wanted to help you. You do not realise the impact you have on people. You are such a great leader Marian, you should believe in yourself."

Marian did not know how to reply to such a compliment. He was right about one thing, she still did not believe that she was capable of leading, and she did not exactly want the ability to lead men to their deaths, fighting her personal battles for her. There was so much she wanted to tell Robin; how much she admired him, and she wanted to get to know him better. She did not know where to start.

They both spoke at the same time. "Robin…"

"Marian, please, I need to say some things. You are so stubborn!"

"No, I am not…" Marian was growing annoyed. What was he trying to get at?

"Just… listen to me. This is hard to say."

"Just say whatever is on your mind." She really did not know him at all. She did not know what to say, or how to act around him.

"Alright, no more lies or secrets. There is a ship taking men to fight in the crusade with King Richard, and I am joining them. They are letting anyone who is able to fight go with them."

"You cannot…" she started.

"Just listen for once in your life!" he snapped at her. "You act like such a child." He paused, blushing. "I am sorry, Marian, I did not mean that. Just let me finish."

"Fine." She tried to sound calm, not childish. He really knew how to get on her nerves.

"I want to go. I want to fight for this country, win the crusade. Come home with King Richard and then he can rescue England from Prince John."

"It is not that simple. Prince John is the better of two evils. The old Sheriff warned me about a man named Longchamp. He holds more power than Prince John."

"I do not care for your politics. I am an outlaw. Why must you always argue with me? I am just trying to do the right thing, for once in my life."

"If that is what you want." She tried to hold back the tears that stung her eyes. He was leaving her again, there was nothing left to say. He did not care about her, not enough to stay.

This new beginning was not going to be as she had hoped.

"In my absence, I am leaving you as leader of my gang. If you do not contact them, I will be instructing them before I go that they should fight for the good of the country. I realise now that outlaws are not the most corrupt, but it is those in power that abuse their authority. If you require the service of my men, Alan will know the methods to find them. Little John and Tobias will lead in your absence. They are your men now."

Marian was too shocked to speak. She let him walk away without another word.

Chapter 30

Gisbourne paced the Great Hall, waiting for his loyal nobles. He had been on edge since he killed the Sheriff two days before. He had prayed that nobody would tell Prince John of his treason and, so far none had betrayed him. Finally, the doors opened. He greeted Ranulf, Earl of Chester. Ranulf was only in his early twenties but it was well known that his own allegiance lay with King Richard. Gisbourne did not trust the Lionheart and his allegiance was more sided towards Prince John, although the nobles had no need to know that information. It was with Ranulf that he had conspired to kill the Sheriff, knowing that those loyal to the King would be more willing, and they in turn had managed to persuade the others that it was the right decision. Now it was a secret they all had to keep. Ranulf was a very bright man and one that Gisbourne did not want to cross. He held great lands within England and with land came power.

The even more respected David, Earl of Huntingdon entered after. He was senior in both rank and age to Ranulf, almost thirty years older than him. He had also recently returned from the Third Crusade having been wounded. He limped a little when he walked as a reminder of his battle. People looked up to him, even others of his rank, because he had proven his bravery and loyalty to his cause. David had been the one to plan the treason and been the power behind persuading the other nobles to stay quiet. The men shared a common interest, as David's wife was Ranulf's sister. They were very close allies as a result and it meant he only had to persuade one to have the other on his side.

"Please sit," Gisbourne gestured. "I would like to thank you for your help in ridding us of the Sheriff. He would have ruined the town with his greed and we need someone who would listen to us, and not enslave us under his rule."

"I agree it was the right decision. But you do know that another will take his place and he could be just as cruel," David pointed out. He had a strong Scottish accent and was in line for the Scottish throne. Gisbourne had to be careful with his words around him.

"I also know that the new Sheriff will be loyal to Prince John but the prince will choose wisely, ensuring Nottingham prospers, and does not grow weak." Both earls nodded in agreement.

"We must tread carefully with this next Sheriff and watch from a distance. Gisbourne, you shall be our eyes and ears. Get close to him and see where his loyalties lie. We must ensure he is what is best for this fair town," said Ranulf.

"Remember, Prince John is keeping his eye on Nottingham as his place of power, so we must be careful. If there is any doubt surrounding the circumstances of the Sheriff's death being caused by a stray arrow, then we may not be safe," warned David.

"Agreed." Gisbourne said. "I will be sure to be seen as completely loyal to the new Sheriff, whatever that entails. I also ask that Marian be pardoned of any crime and be allowed to remain in Nottingham. She was targeted by the Sheriff personally and she should be treated justly."

"That is fair," David agreed. "We must leave before the new Sheriff arrives. No one must know about this meeting. I expect regular reports and ensure your messenger is loyal only to you."

"I will," and at that, they left just as quickly as they had arrived.

#

Marian was finally back home a week after Robin announced he was leaving. He was due to start his journey heading south tomorrow. He had gone back to his men to mourn Will's loss and start the outlaws on a new mission to save England, not add to its blight.

Marian was pleased Robin had finally seen it through her eyes, but just as she had found he was not so dissimilar to his younger self, he was leaving her. She still did not know how he felt for her, but she would wait.

In the meantime, she had a whole gang of outlaws to keep in check, a mammoth task she did not feel prepared for. Robin had not put any pressure on her to deal with them but she did want to make use of them in any way she could. First, she would give them time though, to adjust and to live for themselves. They were preparing for winter and they were behind.

"Marian?" A tap came on her bedroom door, and Alice peered around.

"Come in, Alice. I wanted to speak with you." Marian had not spoken with Alice since her attempted execution. She still could not get her head around why

Gisbourne had killed the Sheriff and not herself, seeing as he had already attempted to kill her before. That was something that could wait for now though. "You are so brave, and so strong. I am sorry for ever doubting you. I would like you to help me take charge of the outlaws. They are preparing for winter and I want you to use up the last of my money left by Walter to help them. They need blankets, food and drink to survive. I know it is nothing that you have trained for, but that time will come. For now, we settle back into our lives and see what the future brings."

"That is all I asked for Marian. It would be my honour."

"Alice, remember. You are not a servant and you never will be. Every decision is yours to make. You are free."

"Thank you, Marian. I have always been free within your household and I will happily serve you for life."

Marian smiled tiredly as Alice left with a new sense of purpose. They were finally at peace and it felt good. She sat by the window, looking out at the world ahead of her.

#

Robin could not bear the guilt of leaving Marian, but he had to get away. He wondered if perhaps he would return to England a different person, or whether he would return at all. He could not help but see Marian one last time before he left. He stood at the entrance to her home, pausing. What would he say to her? But before he had a chance to think it through, Alice opened the door. She looked as shocked as he felt.

"Oh! Sorry, here." She stood aside to let him inside as she left. He had no choice now, he stepped into Marian's home.

Beatrice was in the kitchen area and turned as he walked in. "Marian has been acting strange since you last saw her. Do not stay long if you are here to cause her more pain," she warned him. He ignored her and walked upstairs.

"Marian?" She turned, recognising his voice.

"I did not think you would come to see me again," she replied. She looked so tired.

"I must congratulate you. You have been pardoned by none other than Gisbourne." He attempted to sound casual, relaxed, though seeing Marian made him anything but.

"You cannot be serious. Why would he pardon me?"

"Well, it is the truth. He really must love you."

"Why did you come? To mock me?"

"To be honest, I did not plan to see you again. It just happened."

"Well, goodbye then." She turned away, having lost too many people in one lifetime. He stepped behind her and caressed her shoulders gently.

"I wish I could be here for you, and you probably do not understand, but I have to do this. I cannot promise anything, Marian. Move on and forget about me. There is so much possibility for you, do not lose it all on me." This was the most intimate he had ever been. Marian would not forget about him, ever. She would wait as long as it took, and if he did not return, she would find him, somehow.

"Goodbye, Robin."

THE END